# THE GUN-SHY KID

# THE GUN-SHY KID

Barry Cord

Chivers Press • G.K. Hall & Co.
Bath, England • Waterville, Maine USA

This Large Print edition is published by Chivers Press, England, and by G.K. Hall & Co., USA.

Published in 2002 in the U.K. by arrangement with the author c/o Golden West Literary Agency.

Published in 2002 in the U.S. by arrangement with Golden West Literary Agency.

U.K. Hardcover  ISBN 0–7540–4762–8  (Chivers Large Print)
U.K. Softcover   ISBN 0–7540–4763–6  (Camden Large Print)
U.S. Softcover   ISBN 0–7838–9675–1  (Nightingale Series Edition)

The text of this Large Print edition is unabridged.
Other aspects of the book may vary from the original edition.

Set in 16 pt. New Times Roman.

Printed in Great Britain on acid-free paper.

**British Library Cataloguing in Publication Data available**

**Library of Congress Cataloging-in-Publication Data**

Cord, Barry, 1913–
  The gun-shy kid / Barry Cord.
      p. cm.
    ISBN 0–7838–9675–1 (lg. print : sc : alk. paper)
    1. Missing persons—Fiction. 2. Brothers—Fiction. 3. Large type books.  I. Title.
  PS3505.O6646 G85 2002
  813'.54—dc21                                    2001039967

# THE GUN-SHY KID

# CHAPTER ONE

Kip Nunninger saw it as an empty land—and as a stranger. He had come up between the swaying boxcars just as the sun ran its yellow fingers through that flat and monotonous country that had no characteristic save one—loneliness.

Kip pulled himself up to the top of the boxcar and drew his knees up to his chest as he sat; he tugged his cap over his light blue, squinting eyes. All night the freight train had been laboring through the burnt, broken hills. Now it was on its downgrade run into the long empty valley that faded into nothingness.

The engine's whistle whipped back over the swaying cars, touching a chord of loneliness in Kip.

He flexed his fingers and looked down at his knuckles. He was a lean-hipped, wide-shouldered youngster late from the San Francisco waterfront, and even back there he had been lonely. His brother, and only close kin, had been a bar-room brawler until he had killed a man in a fight and headed east.

Kip had been left in charge of a friend, and when old Jake had died there had been nothing in San Francisco to hold him. He had jumped the first freight heading east out of Frisco, and had come looking for his brother.

1

Fred Nunninger's last letter had been dated over a year ago, and it was postmarked Yellow Horse, Arizona: *'I'll send for you, Kip, as soon as I get started out here. It's big country, kid— most of it empty. I aim to own some of it.'* He had ended the letter with an enigmatic, unexplained line: *'They wear big hats out here, kid . . .'*

Kip still had the letter—it was all he had of his brother. The letter and a memory of a stocky, hard-muscled man with a nose slightly flattened—a rough-hewn face saved from homeliness by a pair of humorously alive gray eyes and a mouth that grinned readily.

Fred and Kip Nunninger had been orphaned early, and Fred, six years older than Kip, had taken over as mother and father and general provider. He had worked on the San Francisco docks, and as a fisherman but he did not like the sea. He had discovered that his hard fists and a hard jaw could earn him money as a fighter and he had gravitated to this—it was in his last bout that he had killed his man and been forced to leave town.

Almost two years had gone by. Kip had stuck it out in Frisco because Jake had needed him more than he had needed Jake. He was twenty plus a few days when he buried the old man and cut his ties with Frisco.

From the grade Kip could see down into the bowl of the valley. Way off to the left in that empty land he made out a splotch of darker green and the specks of several small structures, bunched close around a windmill. Ahead, perhaps five or six miles, a water tower flanked by a small tool shed broke the gray monotony. On the far horizon a long gray ridge placed its indifferent barrier across the iron right of way; the rails went through it in a V-shaped gash.

Kip clasped his hands around his knees and frowned. Up to three days ago he had never been more than twenty miles from San Francisco. The country ahead had no appeal for him, and he wondered what his brother had found out here to hold him.

He knew he was in Arizona, and his brother's earlier letters had mentioned that Yellow Horse was not too far from the SP rails—just where in Arizona, however, Kip had no idea.

His idle gaze caught a movement along the top of the boxcars, and he stiffened slowly. A dark bullet head had come up four cars away. The man was on the iron ladder between cars, only his head showing. The man surveyed Kip with dispassionate intentness; then he ducked down out of sight.

Kip's mouth went grim. He had evaded this brakeman all night, since the last stop in the hills. The railroad man looked like a mean cuss . . .

But the brakeman didn't show up again, and finally Kip relaxed.

3

The freight ran down the long grade and paused briefly at the water tower. The great iron pipe was swung out over the panting engine and gallons of water dropped into the boiler. The steam vents blew white vapor in great hissing broadsides and a tremor went through the long freight line. The engine began its labored grind up the lesser grade toward the ridge pass.

All day the land had been empty and lonely and quiet with a sort of bitter peace. Now early summer thunderheads loomed up before a sudden wind. They came up fast from the far, dark hills, dark-bellied and ominous.

Kip went down the iron ladder between the swaying cars to get away from the threat of rain. He had searched for an empty boxcar last night, but Plug-Ugly, the brakeman, had secured all of them.

Violence came out of the wind and sky and spread over the land; it stirred the latent ugliness in the burly brakeman. Kip was clinging to the partial protection of the ladder between the cars when he happened to look up during a vivid flash of lightning. Through the driving rain he saw the brakeman's broad, beard-stubbled face peering down at him.

'Here's where yuh get off, Jack!' the man snarled. 'The company don't allow no free riders!'

Kip held on with one hand and motioned toward the driving rain. 'You could wait until

4

this lets up,' he suggested grimly. 'I won't cause any trouble.'

'You won't cause no trouble!' the brakeman echoed. His hoarse laughter was drowned in a burst of rolling thunder. He bellied down on the swaying platform above Kip and brought his right arm over. A three-foot hickory club waved menacingly.

'You'll go right now, Jack!' he snarled. 'With a little help from this—'

He swung viciously at Kip's head.

The couplings jolted under Nunninger as he swung away from the blow; his free hand came up smooth as a left jab. His fingers closed around the club and his jerk pulled it from the brakeman's hand.

He tossed it out over the embankment, his eyes narrowing, a pulse of anger beating over his right eye.

'I don't want trouble with you!' he repeated slowly. 'Let me ride through the ridge—'

The brakeman's face disappeared, and Kip wondered if the man had been frightened off. But he reappeared a moment later, outlined against the ominous sky.

This time something glinted in his right hand—a glint that seemed to burst into the long flash of lightning that spotlighted him. He had a cheap, nickel-plated revolver in his hand, and he was tilting the muzzle down toward Kip.

The youngster suddenly had no choice. He

muttered a brief curse at the brakeman as he swung out over the embankment . . . Thunder smothered the pistol's sharp crack but not the small red flare. He felt the burn of the bullet as it cut a gash across his back, and then Kip jumped away from the moving car . . .

He landed on his feet and the momentum threw him off balance; he rolled down into a small muddy torrent racing along the embankment and felt a sharp knife of pain in his left ankle as it twisted under him.

He rolled over and came to his feet and ducked as a red flare winked again from the dark line of cars. He did not hear the report, nor did the bullet come close.

The last car went past him and the red tail lantern winked in the premature dusk. Kip stood up in the driving rain, the grim force of his anger overriding his loneliness. He took a step after the vanishing caboose, and his left ankle gave way and he went down on his hands and knees, a grimace of pain twisting his face.

In the slashing rain he faced the fact that he was afoot and temporarily crippled—and lost. He might well be a hundred miles from the nearest town.

Slowly he crawled back up the five-foot embankment. The rails were the only familar things in this empty land—and back about five miles was the water tower and the shed.

Gritting his teeth, Kip Nunninger hobbled back along the ties.

# CHAPTER TWO

Five miles to the southeast two men waited the storm out in the dubious protection of an abandoned sod shanty. The younger man moved restlessly in the damp gloominess of the interior; the cigaret drooping from the corner of his mouth glowed briefly.

'It was a long shot before, Chinook,' he growled. 'But with this rain'—he made an impatient gesture—'heck, it's a hundred to one he won't show up now.'

The older man had a tobacco quid in his left cheek. He chewed on it morosely, staring out through the hole that was the doorway. Rain made a curtain across it; he could barely see the ten feet to the two horses they had tied to low bushes. The animals were tailing the wind, enduring the rain with stolid patience.

'Westwood'll be there,' Chinook stated. He was a lanky, gristly man with pale gray eyes in a sun-blackened, horsy face. Blond eyebrows made a startling contrast to the blackness of his features. A grease-stained gray Stetson was cocked back on his balding head; two guns were snugged in thonged-down holsters.

The youngster wheeled to face the man in the doorway, his lips thinning. There was a conviction in Chinook's voice that baffled him.

'Just because of a note? Blazes! Give that

Englishman some credit for brains, Chinook!'

'He'll be there,' Chinook repeated. He hunched his shoulders, displeased by the idea of the wet ride facing them. He squinted at the sky, frowned. 'The note told him to be at the tower by sundown. We better be there before he shows up.'

The younger man came to the doorway and glanced at the sky over Chinook's shoulder. There was a long break in the west, and he knew that the worst of the storm was over. He slid his right palm down over the butt of his Colt and rubbed it gently. He was a rather pleasant-looking man, not more than twenty, with a sparse reddish stubble on his chin and upper lip. But there was a weakness to the cut of his jaw, and his blue eyes had a quick-shifting, harried look. He was a man not too sure of himself, or perhaps he did not relish the job ahead too much.

'Heck of a way to kill a man,' he muttered. 'Tricking him like this.'

Chinook turned quickly, eyeing his partner with a narrowing gaze. He had suspected that Vic Canny had no real stomach for this job and now he knew it. Hard lines formed around his tobacco-stained mouth.

'You're gettin' paid for it, Vic. You wanted in on this. Don't go soft on me now!' There was a thin and ugly warning in Chinook's voice that stiffened the other.

'Sure, I volunteered for it!' Vic snapped. 'I

8

wanted a stake to get me to Mexico. You know why—'

'You're gettin' it!' Chinook cut in roughly. 'We do the job an' report back to Kansas, an' you'll have yore money. You can clear out right after.'

'How about you?'

'Me?' Chinook grinned sourly. 'I'm stayin'. I'm cuttin' myself in for more than a few hundred bucks on this deal, Vic. A lot more!' His face was like smooth parchment suddenly crumpled. He chuckled softly. 'There's all of Antelope Valley to be had—an' I'm not settlin' for less than a share of it, a good share of it.'

'Kansas is payin' gun wages, not sharin',' Vic sneered. 'That's what you'll get—or a lead payoff.'

Chinook grinned. 'No, kid.'

Vic's eyes narrowed. 'Why? Why should you be different?'

'Because I know what happened to Brian Westwood,' Chinook answered. He turned and loosed a stream of tobacco juice through the doorway. 'We're ridin' a wet saddle, kid. We better get goin'.'

Beyond the low hill shutting them from sight of the rails, a train whistled. The sound came to them through the rain, a long wail, infinitely lonely.

Vic hesitated. He had a sudden premonition that things were not going to turn out the way Chinook wanted.

9

'I still think we're ridin' on a fool's chase,' he muttered.

The older gunster scowled. 'He'll be there, I tell you. That's all Brent Westwood's lived for these past years—some hope of finding his boy. He'll be there and he'll be alone.'

Vic shrugged. He watched Chinook duck out into the rain, curse harshly as rain seeped down his neck, and mount his dun mare. He wheeled the animal around and looked down at Vic, and the red-headed gunslinger took a hitch at his gunbelt and stepped out.

The rain felt cold against his face, and almost immediately he felt its chill down his neck. He set himself for the unpleasant ride ahead.

The saddle was wet and uncomfortable, and his cayuse, a leggy steeldust, was less docile than Chinook's mount. He had to hold it down with a rough hand.

The long break in the west had now reached across one third of the sky. The rain was lessening perceptibly. If they moved out now they would just make it by sundown.

\*　　　\*　　　\*

The storm played itself out just before Kip Nunninger reached the water tower. Short and violent though it had been, rain had lashed that desolate land as though venting its fury on its hard and unyielding surface. Water ran in a

10

thousand muddy torrents across the sandy earth, only to diminish and vanish altogether a few hours after the storm ceased. By morning little indication would remain that rain had fallen upon that barren and empty land.

Kip was soaked clear through long before he reached the partial shelter of the tower. He crouched in the dry spot by one of the thick supports and watched the drip-off fall in a ring around him.

The wide band of clear sky burst into brilliance as the sun emerged from the edge of the dark cloud mass. Long yellow banners came lancing across the valley, the dark underbelly of the storm clouds took on a violet tone—and from the far reaches of that barren country came a clear, sharp freshness that bit into Kip's lungs.

There was a wild and primitive beauty to this country at the moment that caught Kip's grudging interest. He straightened, feeling the cut across his back as the movement of his muscles pulled against it. Without thinking, he reached in his shirt pocket for his sack of tobacco, and not until he had the soggy bag in his hand did he realize the futility of his gesture. With a wry smile he thrust it back and turned to survey his surroundings.

There was nothing within eyesight except the shining rails which came from the low, ugly hills he had traversed earlier in the day. He followed them with his gaze until they vanished through the cut in the gray rock ridge a dozen miles to the northeast. He had not seen a town since almost a day's ride back—and he had no idea how far he was from one now.

And yet something about the empty land held him; some inner need for elbow room, for reflection. It was a country ideally suited for thinking; it diminished a man in relation to its empty reaches, and yet it challenged him.

It was a land where a man could crawl and die and make no more disturbance than a gnat settling on the surface of a lake; it was also a country where a man could leave his imprint, if he was big enough.

Kip took a deep breath and tried settling his weight on his left foot. He felt pain knife sharply up his leg, and the shock of it twisted the smile on his face into a grimace. Stiffening his will, he hopped over to the shed.

The door was padlocked. He peered through the one dirty window and ran his gaze over kegs of spikes, over picks and shovels ranged along the walls, over lanterns hung on nails. He had expected nothing more, and he was debating whether or not he should break the window and crawl inside to spend the night when he heard horsemen.

There were two of them, he judged, and they were approaching the shed from the other side. He started to move around the small building to meet them, and then some inner caution restrained him.

He heard the jingle of bit irons as the riders pulled up; then a man's flat-toned voice said: 'Keep the hosses in close, Vic. We're just in time. Here he comes now—'

Kip eased his back against the shed, sensing the urgency in that voice. He turned his head and searched the sage-stippled land that stretched toward the west, and he remembered that it was in this direction he had seen the ranch from the top of the freight car. The low sun was full in his face now, but the orb was big and reddening, without power to blind him. Still, he squinted against it, and now he saw a rider emerge from the monotonous pattern of sage and sand and head for the water tower.

The horseman stood tall and erect in the saddle, like some cavalry officer riding past a reviewing stand. He was mounted on a high-stepping, beautiful roan, and he came at an easy canter toward the tool shed.

Then he spotted Kip backed against the shed, pulled the roan broadside and stopped. He was roughly a hundred yards away—a big-boned man wearing a belted, rough tweed coat and tan whipcord britches. With the sun at his back, his face was in shadow and his features were indistinct. He waited, evidently expecting Kip to make some move.

Nunninger heard a muffled curse from the off side of the shed, then a thin whisper:

13

'Somethin's got him scared, Vic. I'm cuttin' around the side. Keep me covered!'

Kip turned quickly. He heard boots crunch on wet gravel. Then a lanky man in range clothes came around the corner of the shed. The man had a rifle in his hands and twin gun belts sagged around his hips. A wide-brimmed hat was cocked down over his eyes.

Curiously, it was the hat that attracted Kip's attention in that moment, recalling a fragment of his brother's letter: *'They wear big hats in this country, kid . . .'*

Then he saw the shock of surprise spread its murkiness across the gunman's pale gray eyes. An ejaculation spilled from the hard, thin lips: 'What in tarnation . . .

Kip started to say: 'Hold it, fella. Count me out of—' He got that much out in a sharp rush of words; then he saw the rifle muzzle swing up and he stepped inside that threatening barrel. His left hand jabbed the muzzle aside; his right crossed smoothly to the gunster's long jaw.

Chinook's rifle went off, the sound spanging sharply across the flats. Moving in, Kip had to throw his weight on his left foot. He grimaced, stifling a cry of pain as his leg gave way. He fell on his hands and knees beside the lanky gunman who lay still, partially twisted over his rifle.

He heard a sharp voice call from the other side of the shed, and he tried to push himself up fast to meet the new danger. He was on one

14

knee when Vic Canny appeared.

The gunslinger pulled up sharply and his Colt jerked up. There was a muzzle blast, Kip saw, an instant after he registered Vic's face in his memory. Then he felt the bullet explode its shock and pain high in his chest and after that he didn't know anything . . .

The rider who had pulled up a hundred yards away suddenly reached for the rifle under his right knee. He laid one shot high, the bullet thunking into the shed over Vic's head. The gunslinger ducked and emptied his Colt at the horseman, hoping to distract the rifleman rather than to score a hit.

One of his slugs scoured a gash across the roan's chest, and the animal reared violently, nearly unseating his rider. For the next two minutes the horseman had his hands full with the frightened animal.

Vic took advantage of the break to call to Chinook, who was coming to: 'Let's get the blazes out of here! Looks like he's had a man planted here to wait for us—no tellin' how many more are staked around!'

Chinook came to his feet, still clutching his rifle. Vic turned and ran around the corner of the shed, and Chinook, still dazed, followed on wobbly legs. Not until he was in the saddle and following Vic did his head clear; then a snarl twisted his lips and his hand dropped instinctively to his holstered Colt.

He had a blurred impression of a strange

15

youngster lying on the wet gravel, and it occurred to him that Vic must have shot him. He eased back in the saddle, but vengeful resentment lingered in him. No man had laid a hand on him since he was fourteen years old.

He spurred his mount alongside Vic's. A long swale had swallowed them from view of the water tower. He thought of the report he would have to make to Kansas, the man who had sent him and Vic on this job, and he licked his lips. He knew the temper of that gun boss.

'Darn you, Vic!' he snarled at the younger man. 'Remember, I'll tell the story! You just back me up!'

Vic turned and looked into Chinook's white face. He saw the fear in the man's eyes, and he felt a chill slide down his back. He nodded. 'Whatever you say, Chinook!'

## CHAPTER THREE

Brent Westwood got the roan under control in time to glimpse the backs of two riders pulling away from the railroad tool shed. He had a few seconds' sight of them before they dipped down out of sight. Then he settled back in the saddle, his face expressionless, his eyes squinting against the deceptive light.

The rim of the sun was sinking behind the hills at his back, and already the colors of the terrain were merging with grayness. The wind was at his back, too; cool with the aftermath of the rain. He steadied the roan and slowly slid his rifle back into its scabbard.

He was a year shy of fifty, this man who for forty-six of those years had pledged his allegiance to another country—to the country of his birth. He was a big-boned man, standing six feet two inches and still solid and erect. His features were square cut, generous, grave. A military mustache, pepper shot, offset the bold hook of his nose, and his hair, ash blond, had grayed and thinned but had altered his looks but little.

He was a man who had grown up with a stiff code of honor, and this had ruled his life. The habit patterns had become an inflexible routine, and he lived by them as unconsciously as he breathed.

He measured the distance to the tool shed with his eyes and studied the shape of the man lying still on the ground before it. He did not know if he had merely stumbled upon a private quarrel, but he rather doubted this. The note he had received had been explicit as to time and place, and it seemed highly improbable that others would have picked this same time and spot to settle a private grudge.

Westwood had come here not unsuspecting, for he had lived three years in this hard and violent land and he knew the forces working against him. But he had come with a thin shred of hope he could never put aside, and for a moment he allowed himself the weakness of a slight sagging of shoulders as he realized he had come on another blind and fruitless appointment.

Three years was a long time to wait, to hope. Yet he knew he would always keep waiting for his son, Brian.

He straightened again, putting his disappointment aside, and his glance steadied on the figure by the tool shed.

'Something went wrong, Tupper,' he said quietly. 'I imagine it must have been a trick to get me here alone, as my foreman warned me. Quite possibly they had a falling out at the last moment. Anyway,' he shook his head, 'there's a chap over there who seems to be hurt.'

The roan nodded. He responded to the name of Tupper, which had been the name of Brent Westwood's valet back in England; the habit of conversation Westwood had started with the valet had continued with his intelligent horse.

He rode slowly, his eyes alert. He made a complete circle around the tool shed and water tower before coming in on the sprawled figure. He saw no other animal tied up nearby, and this puzzled him. Either one of the three men had hidden his horse some distance away, or he had come afoot, which seemed unlikely in this land of long and barren distances.

He dismounted and walked to Kip and

18

stood over him, and a frown spread from his eyes down along the square line of his jaw.

The figure was clad in strange clothes for this country—a black turtle-neck sweater, a peaked cap. He hunkered down by Kip and turned him so he could see Nunninger's face. He noticed the slight froth bubbling on Kip's lips, but it was not blood. Westwood's gaze travelled to the area of blood darkening the bullet-torn sweater high under the collarbone, and he nodded slowly at the slight rise and fall of Kip's breath.

'Not a range chap at all,' he muttered. He turned and glanced at the shining rails, let his gaze follow them to the darkening hills, and the explanation forced itself on him. 'Probably just some tramp who stopped off here at the wrong moment—'

Quite possibly this youngster had saved his life. Westwood considered this as he bent, got his arms under Kip and lifted the youngster's one hundred and sixty-five pounds of dead weight off the ground. He lifted Nunninger easily and carried him to the roan, who skittered away nervously from the limp figure.

'Easy Tupper,' Westwood soothed the beast. 'He's hurt. You won't have to carry him too far—' He mounted with Kip across the front of his saddle and wheeled away. The roan took the double burden patiently. They were still in sight of the tool shed when Westwood saw two riders bob up out of an arroyo and come at a

19

gallop in his direction. He recognized them immediately and turned to meet them.

Vernie Mathis, his foreman, swore with lurid relief as he came up. 'We heard the shots an' came a-runnin',' he growled.

He had been instructed to stay behind at the ranch, but his faith in the senders of the note his boss had received had been nonexistent. He had waited behind just long enough to let his doubts override his respect for Westwood's orders. He had taken Red Powell with him, just in case.

'Ran into trouble, dinja?' he snapped. 'Jest like I said—' Verne usually maintained a reserved and respectful attitude toward his boss, but his relief made him impertinent now, and Westwood overlooked it.

'This chap seems to have received the worst of it,' he said. He glanced at the carrot-topped, slim puncher beside the foreman. 'It's a long ride into town, Red, but I think we should get Doctor Spooner for this fellow. I'll take him to the ranch—it's nearer. Try to get the doctor up to the Three Dot W before morning.'

Red nodded. 'I'll have him there, Mr. Westwood.'

Mathis frowned as he edged his cayuse up close and studied Kip's limp figure. 'Who is he? What was he doin' at the water tower?'

Westwood shrugged. 'Let's get him home,' he suggested. 'Maybe he'll tell us about it—if he lives!'

20

\*　　\*　　\*

Much of the time they were blue, ragged giants wrapped in somber thought, kneeling against the distant horizon. They were old mountains, and their alluvial fans made long gradual slopes into Antelope Valley. Seen through glasses they were rocky and barren, riven by gullies, inhospitable.

They were the Sleepers.

From Brent Westwood's Three Dot W, Kip Nunninger watched them often. Even after he had gotten out of bed and made his way to the chair on the wide, pleasant gallery running the length of the south side of the rambling ranchhouse, he spent much time studying them. He felt the impact of those aloof mountains and a rising excitement as his strength returned.

For he had learned that the mining town of Yellow Horse lay on the far side of those ragged peaks.

He was three weeks mending from the bullet wound. The small hole under his collarbone and the larger, puckered tear under his shoulder blade, where Vic's bullet had emerged, healed quickly, testimony to his youth and vitality.

In the weeks during which he was Westwood's unexpected guest, Kip came to like the big ranch and Brent Westwood.

21

But the life and the problems of the ranch did not touch him; he lived apart from it, avoided by the Three Dot W hands. He was a special guest, to be tolerated until he left. The Three Dot W was an oasis of green in a land of sullen desolation. Creaking windmills sucked water from an underground reservoir, spilling it into small canals and ponds that nurtured grass, trees, flowers and vegetable patches. There was a form and pattern to this ranch, unlike most of the sprawling cattle spreads of the country—an Old World neatness that seemed out of place in this raw, violent land.

Brent Westwood lived alone in the big ranchhouse. An old Mexican housekeeper and her twelve-year-old daughter looked after the place and cooked for him. They lived in a wing of the big house, and after their chores were done kept to themselves.

A strange, lonely man, this Britisher; a man who spent many evenings staring into the flames of his fireplace, wrapped in a brooding silence. He had asked few questions of Kip, and had not probed for the reasons behind Kip's appearance at the railroad water stop.

On the piano in the big living room there was a gold-framed picture of a young man and an older, sharp-faced woman with a wistful smile. It was the only photograph in the house. The woman might have been his wife and the youngster his son, but Kip didn't ask and no

22

information was ever volunteered.

In the time he was at the Three Dot W, Kip never saw Brent play the piano.

There was something bothering Brent Westwood, and it bothered the Three Dot W riders. But it was not Kip's problem, and they did not attempt to involve him in it.

The only man who took a passing interest in Kip was the foreman, Verne Mathis.

He came to the barn where Kip had filled a feed sack with sand and straw and hung it from the rafters, and watched the youngster work the stiffness from his shoulders pounding the makeshift bag. Kip was stripped to the waist, and sweat glistened on his arms and chest.

Mathis stood in the doorway, sucking on a cheroot, his light gray eyes measuring the youngster's shoulders, his quick, sure-footed movement. The kid would be a bad customer to tangle with at close quarters, he thought—but a bullet hit harder and from farther away.

The kid turned and wiped sweat from his face and grinned at him. Verne said: 'Sure hate to be that dummy, kid.' He made a gesture toward the corral. 'I got a cayuse saddled for yuh, if yuh figger yo're ready for him.'

Kip nodded. He picked up his sweater and knotted the sleeves around his throat. His head was bare in the sun and he looked jaunty. ' 'Nother week and I'll be ready to go, Verne. Time, too. I've been hanging around too long.'

Verne shrugged. He handed Kip the reins of

23

a rangy piebald. 'He might be a mite friskier than yo're used to, son. Hold on tight until he works the kinks out. He's jest high-spirited.'

Kip grinned. 'I did some riding back in Frisco. I know how to handle a horse.'

He climbed into the saddle and settled back, and the piebald broke loose. Kip bounced in the saddle, lost his stirrups, and clung to the piebald's neck. The animal kicked its heels a few times and settled into a run, and Kip managed to regain his seat. His face was white when Verne finally rode alongside and headed the piebald back to the corral.

'Figgered he was a mite frisky,' the ramrod said stiffly. He eyed Kip's face. 'That's enough for the day, son.'

Kip shook his head stubbornly. 'Me and him's gotta come to an agreement,' he muttered. 'Let go. I'll give him a chance to work the orneriness out of his system!'

Verne settled back. Kip whirled the piebald around and set him into a run. They left the yard, riding for the low dun hills. The ramrod relighted his cheroot and waited. There were other things troubling him, and Kip meant little to him. The kid didn't belong in this country, and the sooner he left the better for him.

Brent was watching from the veranda, and Verne walked over.

'Kid'll be as good as new in another week,' Verne said. He climbed the stairs and came to stand beside Brent. They looked across the yard to the thin dust banner marking Kip's passage.

'I'll be sorry to see him leave,' Brent said. He was standing with his hands thrust deep in the pockets of his tweed jacket; standing ramrod straight. And there was a hint of wistfulness in his tone.

Verne shrugged. 'Kinda cotton to him myself,' he admitted gruffly. 'But he don't fit in out here. He's young an' cocky, but he don't know what he'll run up against. An' he'll run into trouble the first day he leaves here; trouble he won't be able to handle with his fists.' The ramrod's eyes narrowed and he glanced sideways at his boss. 'He ever say what he was doin' by that water tank?'

'Just waiting,' Brent replied. 'He said he was kicked off the freight which passed, heading east, that afternoon. He was waiting for the rain to let up when they came riding to the tower . . .'

'An' you don't know who they were?' Verne asked the question idly. He had asked it before, and he knew that Brent Westwood would not say because he was not sure.

Brent said nothing, and after a moment Verne picked up the conversation. 'What's the kid out here for, anyway?'

'He's looking for his brother,' Brent said. 'Told me he had no family or relatives save his brother who he believes is in Yellow Horse. He

25

left San Francisco without any money. Hopped a freight heading over the mountains, as he put it, and made a switch south, hoping he'd come within reasonable distance of the gold camp—'

'Ghost camp, you mean,' Verne cut in. He made a disgusted sound. 'Ain't no one up there now, since the mines petered out more than a year ago. 'Bout eight or ten die-hard miners an' some riffraff from the back trails.' His tone grew harsh. 'I wouldn't be surprised if Kansas an' his outlaw crew hang out in Yellow Horse.'

Brent was watching Kip's dust as it veered and began to head back toward the ranch. 'He told me he's quite sure his brother is up there. I hope he finds him, Verne.' Brent's voice was gentle. 'Somehow I hope he finds what he's looking for.'

Verne spat out the soggy remnants of his cheroot. Bluntly he changed the topic to the trouble at hand. 'Red's reported another twenty head gone, up by Fossil Tanks. An' Cozzens' men are stringin' wire around Cold Springs.'

Brent said nothing. Verne's voice held a growing anger. 'They're crowdin' us, Mr. Westwood. We've got to hit back, or Cozzens'll drive us out of Antelope Valley!'

Brent shook his head. 'We have no proof that Monte Cozzens' men are stealing my beef. And as for the fence around Cold Springs, we'll leave that question for the law to judge.

I've no doubt of my prior rights—'

'Law, nothin'!' Verne growled. 'The law's seventy miles away, at Oak Bluffs. Deppity Sheriff Tom Gallen's the nearest thing we've got to law around here, an' he's got more'n he kin handle with Kansas an' his owlhooters raisin' all kinds of Hades. We could be stripped clean an' run out of the valley before the law got around to doin' anythin', Mr. Westwood!'

The Britisher's face held a wooden reserve. 'I have title to the range I own, and title to Cold Springs. I'll not be pushed, Mr. Mathis. But I will not resort to lawlessness. If I did I would be no better than Monte Cozzens. And I'll not risk the lives of my riders to do it.'

Mathis sensed the stubbornness in his employer. He figuratively threw up his hands. 'Yo're the boss,' he growled. 'But I'm warnin' yuh now that the Rockin' V's gonna get tougher. It'll be more than wire fences an' warnin' shots an' a few cows rustled here an' there. They'll push us, Mr. Westwood. I've seen it before. You've got the best spread in this part of Arizona. Cozzens wants it. Some day he'll push us to the point where we can't back away any more. Then it'll be fight—or pull stakes!'

He reached in his pocket and took out a hunk of Old Harmony chaw and carelessly brushed lint from it. He took a healthy bite out of it.

Westwood smiled. 'Cozzens isn't the only bidder for the Three Dot W,' he said. 'I think we're being honored with the presence of Judge Silas Weller again.'

'*Him!*' Verne Mathis squinted toward the road to town. He saw the surrey just as it swung in from the main road and snorted in disgust. 'If that side-show barker ever was a judge I'm a Kentucky Colonel!'

The surrey drew up in the yard, under the willow at the north end of the ranchhouse, and a paunchy man of middle height and age, dressed in black broadcloth, string tie and white shirt, descended. He had silver gray hair carefully combed back, and ruddy cheeks. A white mustache, trimmed short, gave an illusion of strength to a weak mouth. He had a drinker's nose, bulbous, red-veined.

He came to the veranda, brushing alkali dust from his coat. 'Mighty dry trip from town, Mr. Westwood. Mighty dry. Dust gets into a man's throat so he can hardly talk, sir.'

Brent nodded a greeting. 'Perhaps a spot of brandy will help, Judge?'

'It would help indeed,' Silas Weller agreed. He eyed Three Dot W's ramrod warily as he ascended the steps. Verne gave him a cold stare and walked past him.

'Unfriendly sort, your ramrod, sir,' Weller commented. 'Not neighborly at all.'

Westwood's voice held a pointed curtness. 'If you've come to make another offer for my

28

ranch, my answer is still no, sir. I have no intention of selling out.'

'My client's raised his bid to twenty thousand dollars,' Judge Weller said. 'That's absolutely his final offer.'

Brent held the door open for him. 'Perhaps your mysterious client is unaware that the Three Dot W is worth at least five times that amount,' he said coldly. 'I should feel insulted at his offer. And I'm surprised that you are willing to act as intermediary in such an outrageous business.'

Judge Weller gulped. 'I am only acting as broker in this affair, I assure you, sir. However, let me point out that your holdings here are worth only what you can get for them. My client is aware of the trouble between you and the Rocking V. Mr. Cozzens is a hard man and he is employing unscrupulous riders. There is talk in town of a pending range war. In such an event the Three Dot W may be worth even less than what my client has offered you.'

'I'll take that chance, Judge,' Brent replied. He poured two ponies of brandy and watched the old reprobate sip his drink cautiously, then let it trickle down his throat. 'Right smooth brandy, sir,' Judge Weller complimented him. 'I'm sorry that you feel you are not in a mood to sell. If you will pardon me, this is no country for a Britisher. In the event of hostilities with the Rocking V, how sure can you be of the loyalty of your men?'

Brent's eyes held distinct displeasure. 'As sure of their loyalty as I would have been of my son's.' His mouth made a harsh bitter line under his mustache, and for a moment pain showed briefly in his eyes. He took hold of himself, his voice stiff. 'Are you threatening me, Judge?'

Judge Weller poured himself another measure of brandy. 'I'm just pointing out some facts you may have overlooked,' he said smoothly. 'Twenty thousand dollars would—'

'Not even pay for the improvements I've put into the ranch,' Westwood cut in bluntly. 'I'm afraid I must make it quite clear to you, Judge. My answer is no. And I shall not expect you to come here again on behalf of your client. If you wish to pay me a social call, you will be welcome.'

Judge Weller looked like a pouter pigeon as he drew himself up. 'You're making a mistake, sir. I hope you do not soon regret it. However—' He swallowed his brandy and walked to the door.

'Good day, Mr. Westwood. When you run into trouble, then you'll call on me, sir!'

The Three Dot W owner waited, his face stiff as he held back his anger. After a few moments he walked to the door.

Judge Weller was in the surrey, swinging the team around. Kip was just coming into the yard. He rode past the surrey, glancing at the man in the seat. Then he rode on to the corral

30

where Verne waited, and dismounted. His grin was quick, friendly.

'Nice animal,' he said, patting the piebald's dusty neck. 'I think he likes me.'

'He's yores,' Verne said. 'Mr. Westwood wants you to have him. It's little enough, he says, for saving his life.'

Kip flushed. 'Heck, I didn't do anything but get in the way of a bullet.'

The ramrod shrugged. 'That's not his opinion. The cayuse is yores, when yo're ready to leave.'

Kip Nunninger left the Three Dot W five days later. Hitting the makeshift bag no longer brought even a twinge of pain from his shoulder; he could spar five minutes without breathing hard. He felt it was time to go. And thinking this, he felt a faint regret. He had come to like the ranch.

Brent Westwood said goodbye in the ranchhouse. He handed Kip a small buckskin sack containing five twenty-dollar gold pieces. 'I know you're broke,' he said. 'Consider this a loan. And I hope you like the piebald.'

Kip shook the tall man's hand. 'I'll pay you back some day, Mr. Westwood.'

Verne was waiting at the corral. The piebald was saddled, a warbag tied to the cantle. He looked at the youngster standing there, wearing his shapeless gray cap, black sweater, dark brown corduroy pants. The kid's grin was the brightest thing about him.

He shook his head. He was holding a worn cartridge belt rolled around a holster in his hand; the walnut butt of a Colt .45 jutted from it.

He held it out to Kip. 'This is rough country kid,' he said bluntly. 'If yore gonna stick around, you'll need this. Better learn to use it.'

The youngster from Frisco shook his head. 'I ain't mad at anybody.' He smiled. 'I just want to find my brother. He's probably working a mining claim in Yellow Horse. I won't have need for a gun.'

'Take it anyway,' Verne said. He stuffed the belt and gun into the piebald's saddle bag. Turning, he pointed due east. 'Sellout's behind that ridge. Foller the road an' you won't miss it. Good luck, kid. Drop around sometime.'

Kip waved. He put the piebald into a lope and settled down in the saddle. He felt good. Somewhere ahead, in those faraway blue hills, was his brother. He wondered what Fred would say when Kip dropped in on him.

## CHAPTER FOUR

The road followed the rails of the Santa Fe through the grade cut in the mesa flanking Three Dot W's eastern range. The land sloped away on the other side into a vast shallow bowl rimmed by the Sleepers.

Kip pulled up by a small wooden shed flanking the track. New ties were stacked up behind the railroad shack, which was padlocked.

It was a hot day. Patches of cloud, like shreds of white cotton, dotted the sky; the sun burned down over that empty, desolate land.

Kip dismounted, glad to stretch his legs. His backside felt sore and there was a crick in his neck. He worked his shoulders, feeling the sweat sticking his underwear against the small of his back. Sweat itched in his sandy beard stubble.

The sweater was uncomfortable and out of place in this hot dry land, but he had stubbornly refused to conform to the customs of the country. He squinted his eyes against the glare, searching down the long slope for the town Verne had told him would be there.

The piebald snorted and shook his head, bit irons jingling and making a small sound in the stillness. Nothing moved in that sun-beaten land; the silence seemed to press against Kip's ears.

His narrowed gaze found the cluster of shacks at the foot of the slope. Sellout. A strange name for a town, he thought idly. He fished for his tobacco and shaped a smoke, his glance appraising the drab collection of buildings parted by a wide sandy street. He saw that the rails seemed to shun the town. The depot and long warehouse shed on the siding was at least five miles from Sellout. There seemed to be little connection between the two. The rails continued on across the monotonous gray emptiness, fading into the glaring distance where the broken southern spur of the Sleepers stood silent guard.

Kip's gaze reached out across the shimmering flats toward the distant hills. He had an awesome awareness of vastness and incredible loneliness; the town in the hollow below seemed a lost and inconsequential thing in the desolate country.

*Wonder what Fred found out here to keep him?* he reflected, and tried to summon up a picture of the brother who had been father and mother to him. But the effort brought only a blurred image of a hard-jawed man with a slow, crooked smile; a brother who had been stern and yet affectionate—a man ruled by some inner violence.

'It's a big country out here, kid,' he had told Kip the night before he left. His broken-knuckled right hand had fisted, as though he wanted to take hold of it. 'A man can get somewhere, if he's got the guts and the fight in him! I'll send for you as soon as I get settled. Until I do, stick around with Jake. He needs you, kid.'

The piebald nuzzled him now, breaking in on his reverie, and he turned to the animal, instinctively warming to the cayuse. 'It's big country all right, Dusty,' he muttered, 'Real big. Kinda like it myself. A man can see far out here—'

He flicked the butt of his cigaret away and climbed into the saddle. The sun was lowering over the ragged horizon behind him, but the heat lay still and implacable over the slope. He grinned. 'Let's take a gander at this flea-bitten town in the middle of nowhere . . .'

Deputy Sheriff Tom Gallen came out to the doorway of the Territorial House, anger making him restless and irritable. His left arm was in a sling, and his gray eyes had a dark brooding look as he surveyed the result of yesterday's raid on the bank.

Kansas and his owlhooters had struck at high noon. Siesta time. Eight hard men, filtering through town slowly. From the east and west—through the north and south alleys.

Most of Sellout was asleep. Even the dogs lay panting in the scant noon shade.

He remembered that he had been caught dozing in Tony's barbershop. Tony had just finished shaving him; he lay tilted back with a hot towel on his face, feeling for the moment at peace with himself and with the world. He had heard the converging riders and some warning had stirred in the back of his mind. But it had been quiet in the shop, with only the drone of flies making any sound. He had closed his eyes and let the warning filter from his head.

Not until shots racketed in the sun-beaten

street did he recall the converging riders. He had whipped out of the chair and charged for the door, his Colt nestling in his fist, only to run into a burst of gunfire from a rider in the middle of the street—shots which had spun him around and dropped him across Tony's doorway.

He realized now that they must have checked and spotted him in the barbershop and had a man waiting for him. Morosely he conceded that he had been lucky yesterday afternoon. He had a smashed collarbone and a gash across the upper arm. It could have been worse.

Now he stared sourly at the wreckage of what had been Crawford's Territorial Bank's brick front. There had been a lot of belated shots fired, and several Sellout citizens had needed patching by Doctor Spooner. One of them, Abe Mosher's eighteen-year-old son who had come out of Abe's store to see what the excitement was about, had taken a bullet in the head and was laid out in Doctor Spooner's back room mortuary.

The bank was closed while Benjamin T. Crawford took stock of his affairs. How much Kansas had taken from the bank was not yet generally known, but Crawford wore a white, grim face. He had asked for, and Tom Gallen had agreed to, a week's moratorium while he straightened out his finances.

The deputy's glance moved idly along the

street and jumped to the mesa trail which he could see distinctly from where he stood. There was a rider heading for town, and his eyes narrowed against the lowering sun. Coming from that direction, the rider was probably a Three Dot W man.

Three Dot usually rode into Sellout in a body these days, he remembered. And he frowned, feeling greatly tired and put upon. Tom was a tall, gaunt man, hardened and tempered by the country, and he took his deputy sheriff's badge seriously. He was a man about forty years old; he had been married and found it not to his liking. The separation had been by mutual accord. He liked his own company best and he felt no loneliness. When he desired feminine company he knew where to go.

His gaze ranged the wide, sandy street bisecting the shabby town. A half-dozen horses nosed the tie-bar of the Three Deuces Bar. Rocking V brand. He hoped Three Dot wouldn't ride in today. The feelings between the two Antelope Valley spreads were strained to the breaking point.

Gallen felt tired and inadequate as he considered this. Kansas' bold raid still rode him with rough spur. With him gunshot and out of commission, a half-hearted posse had taken off after the bank robbers, only to run into an ambush in the Sleepers. They had straggled back, shame-faced, sullen.

Crawford had muttered something about sending for bank detectives—asking help of the Arizona Rangers. Tom Gallen smiled at this. He knew Crawford would get little outside help. The law was scattered too thinly over that empty land.

Now he put his cold regard on the gunman who came thrusting out of the Three Deuces and went swaggering up the street. Tom knew him as Vic Canny. He and an older, lanky man Tom had heard called Chinook were new riders for Cozzens' Rocking V. He distrusted both of them. They had the earmarks of owlhooters. But a search through the dodgers in his files brought up nothing on them, and he couldn't jail a man on an unfounded suspicion.

He watched Vic turn into the Bonnie Bonnet Lunch-room, and it occurred to him that it was more than food that was arousing Vic's interest. Sally Mason, he reflected dourly, was a pretty dish.

Thinking of the girl in the lunchroom started his thoughts on the nagging mystery of Brian Westwood.

He had known the young Britisher only slightly. Brian had come here more than three years ago, to take over Three Dot W until his father Brent arrived. Three Dot had been owned by Sir Gerald Westwood, Brian's uncle, and run by Verne Mathis. Sir Gerald had come to visit Three Dot only twice in the years before his death, and then only to use its

38

facilities as a camp for hunting expeditions in the nearby hills.

Sir Gerald had been lucky, Tom Gallen reflected, for he had left the running of Three Dot to Verne Mathis—and Verne was an honest man. With another man managing Three Dot, Brian Westwood might have taken over a stock-stripped, run-down ranch.

Brian had come to Arizona from England six months before his father, Brent Westwood. Tom Gallen understood that the elder Westwood had remained behind to straighten out legal and personal matters, and in that period his wife had died. He had intended to look over his inheritance from his brother, Sir Gerald, and return to England with his son, Brian. His son's disappearance held him now, tied to this lonely grim land by an undying hope.

Brian, Tom remembered, had seemed to shed his British ways and stiffness remarkably quickly. He had been tactful over at Three Dot; he had not interfered with Verne Mathis. He had quickly changed to range garb and seemed to delight in wearing a belt gun. He was a fair shot, but soft; he had shied from open conflict and taken the rough banter of the tough element. In time they had let him be.

At the time of his disappearance he was seemingly interested in Sally Mason who, by her own admission, had liked the young British

39

heir. Sally Mason ran the Bonnie Bonnet Lunchroom with her widowed mother, and Brian's interest in her had been a feather in her cap.

At the same time Brian had been paying courtly attention to Meg Havison, youngest of three spinster sisters who lived alone on the old Gunner Havison homestead.

Gunner Havison, mountain man and Indian fighter, had pioneered Antelope Valley with old John Straw, who owned the livery stables and who had named the town in bitter resentment at the railroad's refusal to meet his price on a right of way. Santa Fe had accordingly laid its tracks away from town, and Straw had shrugged and settled back in the indifference of old age.

Havison could have owned Antelope Valley. When he died, drunk, rolled and knifed in Three Deuces' back alley, he had left his motherless daughters a run-down ranch on Devil's Fork where Diablo Creek ran underground to provide an underground lake for Antelope Valley; and an unshaken belief that they should own Antelope Valley.

Gallen frowned as the run of his thoughts took him back to the night Brian had disappeared.

The young Britisher had come to town and chatted with Sally Mason. Sally later said that Brian had received a note while he was there. She didn't know whom it was from, and the old man who had brought it to him had come while she was busy in the kitchen. She had only glimpsed him leaving.

Brian had left right away. It was about nine o'clock in the evening. He had walked out—and disappeared!

His gelding was still at the rail the next morning. A check of the depot revealed that he had not taken a train from there. Nor had he hired another animal from John Straw. No one remembered seeing him. Yet he was not in town.

It had been speculated that Brian might have taken a freight out of the valley. But that made no sense. Young Brian had been expecting his father the first of the week. He would not willingly have left without a word of explanation, without any preparation.

But to this day there had been no trace of Brian Westwood. Brent Westwood had searched high and low. He had hired detectives, and finally retreated to the Three Dot to wait.

A trickle of sweat came down Gallen's stubbled cheek and he lifted his good hand to brush it away. It was a mighty hot day, he thought gloomily. His shoulder pained him. But he had the unwelcome hunch that the day would get worse, and it soured him. He wondered why he remained here in this God-forsaken town in the middle of empty rangeland, wearing a star which endangered

41

his life daily for one hundred and fifty a month.

The rider from the mesa trail was in town now, jogging his piebald down the dusty street. Tom Gallen measured him with cold eyes, and a sneer curled his lips while his gaze held a thin surprise.

He had seen all kinds of men drift into and out of Sellout in the eleven years he had been the law there. This one was the strangest.

A cocky youngster in the dangedest getup he had ever seen on top of a horse. A black turtle-neck sweater which was probably practically killing him in this heat. A shapeless gray cap, bill tugged down over his eyes. A boy probably not even twenty years old, with the stiff seat of a man unused to riding long distances. No belt gun: No rifle. In Antelope Valley, Tom mentally observed, this was tantamount to an alarming lack of foresight.

Kip Nunninger jogged past the deputy, and Tom Gallen caught the full impact of a pair of level, light blue eyes. Those eyes measured Gallen with a cool regard and with a hint of amusement, as though the rider were seeing an oddity. Gallen felt the back of his neck burn under the kid's stare.

But something familiar jogged at his memory. He remembered now that he had seen someone like this youngster before— someone dressed like him who had passed through Sellout. Two, or was it three years

42

ago? A heavier, more powerfully muscled man, shorter, but with the same sort of features ...

Gallen watched the youngster ride by him and pull up before the big barn at the far end of town. Old John Straw was sitting on a bench in front of the building.

John Straw sucked on his unlighted corncob. He eyed the rider pulling up by the manure-littered ramp with the sharp scrutiny of age, with the air of a man who has seen a lot and is surprised by nothing.

Kip leaned forward in the saddle, resting his forearms on his pommel. 'Howdy, old-timer.' He waved a hand, encompassing most of the town. 'Looks like a reg'lar war's been going on.'

'Has been,' Straw grunted. His eyes narrowed, the skin folds crinkling deep. 'You one of them?'

'One of who?'

'The galoots who robbed the bank.' John Straw didn't seem perturbed. 'Reckon not,' he answered himself. Then his voice sharpened. 'What in tarnation you rigged up for? Dangedest-lookin' range clothes I ever clapped eyes on!'

Kip was nettled. 'They're good enough for me,' he muttered. He glanced up the street. 'Bank holdup, eh? You're taking it easy enough.'

'Don't keep my money in the bank,' the

oldster said calmly. 'Don't have any money, anyway—saves me a heap of worryin'.' He cocked his head on one side, like a scrawny hen sizing up a bug. 'Reckon you want that piebald put up for the night.'

Kip nodded. 'I'll need him in the morning. I'm traveling early.' He slid out of the saddle.

'Three Dot W cayuse,' Straw said, rising. He knuckled his knobby nose speculatively. 'You don't look like a boss thief, son. But I never knowed Verne Mathis to be generous with Three Dot cavvy.'

'He ain't,' Kip retorted. 'Happens Mr. Westwood loaned me the cayuse himself. Now if you'll just point out the nearest eating place in town, I'll turn Dusty over to you.'

'That'll be a dollar four bits. In advance.' John Straw held out a horny hand. 'Just in case Mathis rides in an' doesn't recollect his boss loanin' no stranger this piebald.'

Kip dug out a gold piece and handed it to the oldster, who calmly bit into it with stubby teeth. He dug into his pocket and drew out a worn snap-purse and took out change.

'The Bonnie Bonnet's 'bout the only eatin' place in town.' He pointed with his pipe stem. 'See it? Place with the curtains in the winder. Never eat there myself, though,' he added. 'Cook my own grub—'

'And wash your own dishes,' Kip gibed softly. 'You're welcome to it, Pop. Take good care of Dusty for me.'

'Better care than you'll get, bub,' Straw snapped. He watched the youngster head across the street, and then he glanced toward the Territorial House where deputy Tom Gallen made a long dark shadow.

'Wouldn't have yore job for the world, Tom,' he muttered. 'No sirreee!'

## CHAPTER FIVE

Kip crossed the street and headed back along the plank walk. He noticed that the deputy sheriff was still eyeing him from the doorway of the Territorial House, and he caught the sullen glances of passers-by. The heat pressed down over this shabby town and he felt its weight on him; he licked his lips and found them paper dry.

Unconsciously he straightened his shoulders and put jauntiness into his stride. The town's troubles were no concern of his. He'd be gone in the morning, and he didn't think he'd ever be back.

Print curtains, faded by the harsh sun, made a backdrop for the sign painted on the big window: BONNIE BONNET LUNCHROOM, Mae Mason, Prop. He opened the door and stepped into a room that was several degrees cooler than the street. A bell worked by a door cord jangled somewhere in the kitchen behind the serving counter.

At this hour the place was almost empty. Kip glanced around the neatly swept ten-by-fourteen room with fly-paper dangling from the ceiling. A fly buzzed angrily, trapped in the goo. Water had been recently sprinkled over the scrubbed board floor; its coolness was in the air.

A man sat at the counter, his back to Kip. A lean young red-necked man with copper hair growing long down his neck was talking to a girl behind the counter. A wide-brimmed gray Stetson was cocked back from his forehead. His voice had a sharp, almost demanding quality.

'I asked you first, Sally. Won't let anyone else take yuh—'

'I'll go with whom I please!' the girl snapped. She had her hand on the counter. She started to draw back, but the customer clamped a hand over hers, holding her.

'I asked you first!' he said roughly. 'Won't have you goin' to that dance with anyone else. Remember that!'

She jerked her hand free, and then her glance lifted to Kip, coming in, and she put a false smile on her face. Kip saw that she was young, pink-cheeked and blue-eyed; her hair was soft brown and tied back in a loose tail on her shoulder.

She said: 'Good afternoon, sir. May I help you?'

46

Kip was almost at the counter. The man still had his back to him; he was hunched over his coffee cup, scowling, evidently not giving a continental who had entered.

But Kip knew him. Even from the back he knew this lean, red-headed man with the big gray hat and the bone-handled guns jutting big and dangerous at his hips. The day was suddenly less pleasant, and anger crawled through Kip.

He reached over and tapped Vic Canny on the shoulder. His voice was soft, like steel encased in kid gloves. 'Howdy, Mac. I've got something for you—'

Vic swung around on his stool, temper glinting in his eyes. 'Who in the devil—'

Kip slapped him. He rocked his head back with the sharp blow and brought his arm back in a backhanded swipe across Vic's mouth. It was fast and hard and it split Vic's lips and brought a glaze to his eyes. Then the gunman spat out a surprised curse and lunged off the stool, his right hand jerking down for his holstered Colt.

Kip hit him again, this time a solid smash to the mouth. Vic started to sag. His fingers groped aimlessly for his butt. Kip hit him again, two quick, fluid blows, his shoulder muscles rippling to the drive of his arms. Vic jarred hard against the counter, rattling his coffee cup. He bounced off, and Kip hit him behind the ear as he fell.

Vic slammed into the floor face first, bounced a little, lay still. His hand had drawn his Colt; his fingers were curled around the butt. His hat had come off his head and lay beside him.

Kip toed the man gently and made a clucking sound. He picked up Vic's hat and set it on the counter beside his cup and slid onto the stool beside it, his smile innocent. 'Big hat,' he said, à propos of nothing. 'Kinda gives a man the wrong impression.'

The girl found her voice. 'You know what you've done?'

He shrugged. 'Put a couple of lumps on a loudmouth's jaw.' He grinned at the look on her face. 'In case you're wondering, ma'am— he had it coming. We ain't exactly friends.'

She drew a sharp breath. 'You dumb, baby-faced, witless fool! And it isn't ma'am,' she said in a rush; 'it's Miss Mason. Sally Mason. And if you don't get out of here right away, he'll—'

'Why, Sally,' Kip chuckled, 'he ain't going to do a thing. He's taking it a lot easier than you are.'

Color flamed in her cheeks. She came around the counter and looked down at Vic; she knelt beside him and took the Colt from his exposed holster and tugged the other from his limp grasp. She straightened, turning to Kip who was watching from the stool. 'You fool!' she repeated tensely. 'I don't know who you are and I don't care. But I don't want anyone killed in my place.' She pointed one of Vic's guns at him. 'Now wipe that silly look off your face and get out of here!'

Kip saw that she was serious. He sobered, looked down at the red-headed Rocking V puncher, shrugged. 'I don't intend to get killed, Sally. If you'll calm down a bit and listen—'

'I've been listenin'!' a quiet voice said. 'Mebbe you better do what Sally says!'

Kip raised his glance to the man pushing into the room. The girl whirled and her hands dropped to her sides. Relief came into her voice.

'Tom! I'm glad you're here!'

Tom Gallen came into the room to stand over Vic Canny. Close up, Kip saw that the deputy sheriff was a long-shanked, gaunt man with piercing dark eyes, receding brown hair. A solid man, honed down by work and worry. There was an uncompromising harshness around Tom Gallen's mouth that indicated there was little humor in the man.

Vic was beginning to stir. He groaned and rolled over, but his eyes were still glazed. His mouth was bleeding and puffed and there was a robin's egg lump behind his right ear.

Gallen put his gaze on Kip. 'A troublemaker, eh?' His voice was low, bitter.

'Just a minute, Sheriff,' Kip said coldly. 'I owe this gent more than a couple of belts on

49

the side of the jaw. But I'm willing to call it even, if Carrot-top here does, too.'

Gallen looked down at Vic, who was stumbling to his feet. The Rocking V puncher staggered and put his hands on the counter and turned slowly, leaning his weight against the wood. His eyes raked Kip with dawning recognition; humiliation twisted his mouth.

'Never saw the fool before, Sheriff,' he said harshly. His words were chewed between his split lips. 'I was sittin' here, mindin' my own business, when he pussyfooted up behind me an' clouted me!'

'You're a two-faced liar!' Kip growled. 'You've seen me before. Up by the water tower, west of the mesa. On Three Dot W range.'

Vic pushed his shoulders away from the counter and dropped his hands to his gunless holsters. He turned and glared at the girl. 'Give me my guns! I'll teach this freak to call me a liar—'

Kip started for him. Gallen put a heavy hand on Kip's shoulder and jerked him around. 'That's enough—from both of you!' he said coldly. He pushed Kip back to his stool and eyed him with frowning speculation. 'You saw Vic before?'

Kip's eyes were blue chips of ice. 'I saw him, and his horse-faced partner. I was minding my own business, keeping out of the rain, when they showed up at the water stop. I can't blame them for being surprised at seeing me. But this yahoo tried to kill me—'

Vic tried a grotesque sneer.

Gallen said grimly; 'You can prove this?'

'Mr. Brent Westwood will back me up,' Kip said. 'So will Verne Mathis and the rest of the Three Dot W boys. I've just put in four weeks recovering from the slug he put into me.'

The deputy sheriff turned to Vic. 'What were you doing up at that water stop on Three Dot W range, Vic?'

Vic wiped his bloody lips with the back of his hand. His eyes glinted. 'If you're fool enough' to believe this bum's story—'

'It ain't a story,' Kip snapped. 'Way it happened, he and his horse-faced partner were waiting to kill Brent Westwood. I just happened to be there at the wrong time—'

'You gonna stand there an' listen to the fool, Sheriff?' Vic's voice was harsh.

Tom frowned. 'I'm listenin'. I'm listenin' to you, too, Vic. What were you an' Chinook doin' on Three Dot W range?'

Vic turned and picked up his hat from the counter. He jammed it on his head. His voice was ugly. 'If you're gonna believe a bum, then I'm through with you, Sheriff! An' if you want me to make somethin' out of it, you know where to find me! Me an' Chinook will be in the Three Deuces—'

He turned to Sally. 'I'll be back for my Colts.' He walked past Tom Gallen, who didn't

51

try to stop him. His swagger didn't quite come off. Without his guns, Vic Canny didn't seem quite so formidable. He looked like a thin, reedy boy who had grown up too fast.

He turned at the door. 'You better be out of town before sundown, fella.' His voice was pitched low, but a bitter hatred burned in it. 'Or get yoreself a Colt. 'Cause yo're gonna need it!'

Sally Mason sighed. The tension drained out of her and she sagged back on a stool, holding out Vic's guns to Gallen. 'I took them from Vic when he was unconscious, Tom. I didn't know what he'd do when he came to.'

Kip turned to her. 'I'm much obliged, Sally. He might've tried to use them—'

'Use them?' Gallen's voice was an impatient growl. 'Who in the devil are you, kid? An' what's the whole story about Vic an' Chinook shootin' you last month?'

Kip shrugged. 'I'm Kip Nunninger. Never been outside San Francisco until I came out here. Grew up on Sand Street, weaned on Paddy's Wharf. An orphan. Was brought up by my brother who left Frisco four years ago. Kinda brought myself up after that. I knew how to tack a sixteen-foot yawl across the Bay before I was fourteen. Learned to handle my dukes in Pat Malone's gym, on Market Street. Fought under the name of Kid Malone. Had more than twenty bouts under my belt when I hopped a freight to come out here and find my brother.' He slacked off then, grinning. 'That's me—Kip Nunninger.'

He told Gallen about being kicked off the freight and about the incident at the water stop.

'I know who I saw,' he insisted. 'Horse-faced man, older than Vic, and Vic. I can't swear they were waiting to kill Mr. Westwood. But they tried to kill me!'

Tom's eyes were dark with reflection. 'Vic swears that he never laid eyes on you before, an' I reckon Chinook will tell the same story. I can't hold them on yore word alone. Can't understand what they'd be doin' on Three Dot range. Both men work for Monte Cozzens' Rocking V spread. Come to think of it, it ain't been three weeks since Monte hired them—'

He shook his head. 'They're hard customers, son.' He glanced at Kip's gunless hips. 'You packin' a hideout?'

'Hideout?'

'Sleeve gun? Derringer?' Tom's voice was impatient.

Kip shook his head. 'Mathis gave me a shell belt and gun; I've got it in my saddle bag. Don't know how to use it, Sheriff.'

Gallen threw up his hands. 'Then get out of Antelope Valley, pronto. That's good advice. This is rough country. If you get in a fight here, you don't settle it with fists. A man carries a gun, an' he uses it. I'm the law here, but I can't be everywhere. Sometimes a man

53

has to be his own law. Get out of Antelope Valley—and don't come back unless you learn to use one!'

Kip shrugged. 'I'm a peaceful man, Sheriff. An' I don't plan on staying.'

Tom nodded. 'I heard Doc Spooner tell he'd gone up to Three Dot to patch up somebody. I thought it was one of Westwood's regular hands—' He turned at the door. 'I'll keep an eye on Vic tonight. Get yourself a room in the Territorial House an' turn in early.'

Kip grinned. 'I'll get the room, Sheriff. And I promise I'll be on my way at sunup!'

'I'll see that you are!' Tom Gallen, growled, and slammed the door behind him.

Kip swung around on the stool and put his cap on the one beside him. 'Sort of worked up an appetite, miss. ' He grinned. 'What's on the menu?'

Sally looked at him. His infectious grin gave him a boyish look; he looked so incongruous in the black turtleneck sweater that her mouth softened and she almost smiled.

She got up, tossed her head. 'Hash,' she said, and walked back to the kitchen.

Kip looked at his skinned knuckles. The afternoon had worn away and the sun was gone from the street. A couple of customers came in and sat at the counter; they looked at Kip with frank, wondering scowls.

He sat apart, not particularly caring.

54

Sally came out of the kitchen just as a stout woman with white hair came into the lunchroom. Sally smiled and said: 'Hello, Ma—it's slow tonight,' and brushed hair from her face.

The older woman nodded briskly. 'I'll take over, Sally.' She went around the counter and disappeared into the kitchen.

Sally set a heavy glazed plate in front of Kip and brought him a mug of coffee. Kip said: 'What happened in town? Bank looks dynamited—'

'The bank was held up and robbed yesterday, by Kansas and his outlaws!' She looked at him in a speculative way, as if trying to appraise his interest. 'Doesn't mean anything to you, does it?'

He shrugged. 'Should it?'

Her lips tightened. 'A lot of people in town and in the Valley may be affected,' she said coldly. 'Mr. Crawford will feel the loss. But our funds were not insured—'

'Yours?'

'We had some savings,' she said sharply. Then she relaxed. 'It isn't going to make things easier for me, blaming you for not taking it the way I do. I'm sorry. From what you told Tom Gallen, you haven't exactly been given a royal welcome to our valley.'

He grinned. 'I ain't mad at anybody for it. What happened to me was probably a mistake. And I took my satisfaction for it, on the man who shot me.' He shrugged. 'I hope Kansas is caught and you get your money back—all of you.'

She moved away to serve the others, and when she went into the kitchen Kip rolled himself a smoke. It was getting dark. Sally came out and lighted the two wall lamps, and Kip helped her with the overhead counter light.

He lingered over his coffee, hoping she'd leave and he could see her home.

But other customers kept coming in, and she stayed. He watched her, liking the way she walked, the way she held herself. Even when the place began to fill up and she was rushed she kept her good humor. She moved swiftly and made small talk without coyness. There was a directness about this girl that interested him.

He paid for his meal during a lull in her activities. 'You know,' he said impulsively, 'I'm sorry I'm leaving. I'd like to eat here again.'

She smiled. 'Any time you're in Sellout, Mr. Nunninger.' Her laughter bubbled out. 'Unless you cook your own, you'll have to eat here.' Her eyes sobered. 'Stay away from men with big hats, Kip—and guns. And I hope you find your brother—'

She moved away again, and he turned to the door. He paused to let two men come in. One of them was saying: 'There'll probably be trouble tonight. Just saw Verne Mathis an' a

56

coupla Three Dot riders come by.'

Kip caught Sally's quick look at him as he went out.

## CHAPTER SIX

Deputy Tom Gallen lived in a small cramped room behind the law office which was on the corner of the main street, strangely called No Water Avenue, and Dobson's Alley. The office building was a long, narrow adobe structure which had been a warehouse and was converted now to the law's uses. Between the front office and Gallen's living quarters was a cell block containing two cubicles, each with a small barred window and an iron-barred door. The doors helped to give what ventilation there was to the small cells.

He had not eaten since noon, and then only a sandwich, but he did not feel hungry. He stood in the darkened doorway, feeling a small gnawing pain in his shoulder. Things had been quiet in town recently, except for the raid on the bank, and there was no one in the cells. When he had a prisoner he was authorized to employ a jailer, and he generally called on Stump Peters, a peg-legged Civil War veteran who eked out his part-time salary by working for John Straw as stable handyman.

His thoughts went back to the raid yesterday

as though drawn by a bitter magnet. He had sent a letter to the sheriff's office at the county seat, explaining what had happened, and his helplessness as far as Kansas and his owlhooters were concerned. He had taken pains to frame his message, for he was not fluent with words. He had ended with a blunt appeal for help:

'I've got a range war brewing, too. Need help. If you could get the Governor to authorize it, I could use a couple of Rangers.'

He didn't expect too much to come of his letter, but he had explained his helplessness here, and there was nothing more he could do.

Gallen reached in his vest pocket for his last cheroot and lighted it. Standing in the doorway of his office, he could see both ends of town. Sellout was small enough so that he knew its every mood, every angle of its buildings, every person in it.

He saw Pat Kelly come out of the doctor's office with Doc Spooner in tow. Pat was nervous and moving with quick, choppy strides, gesticulating. Doc Spooner was carrying his black bag and buttoning his coat as he hurried beside the smaller man. Gallen knew that Kelly's wife was sick again.

Monte Cozzens, owner of the Rocking V, showed up on the far walk. He was a squat, burly shadow, but Gallen recognized him and a faint surprise went through him. Judging from the direction from which Monte had come, the deputy guessed that the Rocking V boss had been to see banker Crawford. Crawford owned a modest place behind town, in a small hollow with a spring and cottonwoods. He had bought the place a few years ago from Tully Albright, hoping to make a home for his wife who was ailing with lung fever. It was the reason for Crawford's being in Antelope Valley in the first place, his wife's ailment. But she had died a year ago last May.

Tom had thought Crawford would give up then, but he had remained on. He had two children, a boy and a girl, aged ten and twelve.

Gallen speculated briefly on Monte's reason for visiting Crawford. As far as he knew Monte didn't have a note with the bank.

He watched Monte cut away from the building line and cross at an angle to the Three Deuces. He hoped Monte would be rounding up his men for the trip home. He sucked on his cheroot, his thoughts drifting to the kid who had manhandled Vic Canny, and to the implications of Kip's accusations. If Vic and Chinook had been hired to ambush Westwood, who was to benefit? Monte was the most likely person. But he hadn't figured Monte that way. A stubborn man with a temper and not too many scruples, perhaps; but not a man to hire killers from ambush.

Judge Weller then? The man was obviously a phony—a front for some mysterious client whose name he refused to divulge. He had

59

come into Sellout a month ago with the avowed intention of looking over ranchlands for his client. Three Dot W and Rocking V were the only ranches of any size in the valley; there were a half-dozen hole-in-the-wall outfits farther north.

Weller had approached Rocking V, Gallen knew, and been run off the ranch. He had been up to see Westwood, but the deputy didn't know what had happened there; he was not on friendly terms with Westwood. Nor on bad terms, either, he thought bleakly. It was just that Westwood was an aloof sort who seldom came to town and was not one for passing the time of day. Still, Verne and the other Three Dot riders must like him. They were a loyal, clannish bunch.

He remembered now that Judge Weller had come back from Three Dot and almost immediately had driven off again. Whoever his client was, he kept the man well heeled. Weller lived in the Territorial House and he paid his drinking bill at the Three Deuces, which Gallen knew to be considerable.

Gallen sighed. He didn't like problems. He was a direct man, a blunt man, and he liked to face his troubles squarely. Kansas he could understand, although he was without power to do anything in that direction. But this trouble between Rocking V and Three Dot required diplomacy and persuasion, and he was no hand at this.

The cigar glowed in his mouth. He saw that the animals at the Three Deuces rail were getting restless. They had been tied up there for the better part of the afternoon. Inside the saloon it was quiet; Rocking V was not boisterous this evening.

He might turn in early, he thought. His arm wasn't feeling too good. He took the short stub of the cheroot from his mouth, and then he saw riders loom up at the western edge of town, and the sense of peacefulness left him and he swore in bitter frustration.

Verne Mathis, trailed by two Three Dot W riders, came by. They were obviously headed for the Three Deuces. Gallen stepped out into the street, his voice lifting sharply in the night.

'Verne!'

The lead rider pulled up and the others swung aside to avoid a collision. Mathis looked back to the tall figure moving toward him. He was a silent shadow, waiting.

'Rockin' V's in the Three Deuces!'

'So-o-o-o?' Verne's drawl held a cool question.

'There's been enough trouble in town!' Tom Gallen snapped. 'Kansas held up the bank yesterday. I ain't in the mood for more shootin'.'

'We don't aim to cause trouble, Tom,' Verne cut in thinly. 'Are you tryin' to tell us that Rockin' V has priority on the likker in town? Are you barrin' us from the Three Deuces?'

Gallen's mouth tightened harshly. 'If it means trouble, I am, Verne!'

The Three Dot ramrod scowled. 'Tom, don't force my hand. Three Dot's played square with the law. We've caused you no trouble before. Don't take sides now. Don't play Monte Cozzens' game.'

'I play no game but my own,' Gallen answered stubbornly. 'But Rockin' V's in the Three Deuces. If you an' yore men walk in there now—'

'We intend to,' Verne said bluntly. 'I want to see Monte anyway, about some wire he's stringin' around Cold Springs.'

'That so?' Gallen said dismally. His right hand came up and his Colt muzzled the shadowy men. 'Get down out of saddle, all of you!'

Verne looked down at that faintly glinting muzzle. His eyes were angry slits. 'So that's how it is, Tom?' he murmured bleakly.

'Get down! Don't force me to use this!' Tom's voice was bitter.

They dismounted.

'Walk yore cayuses up here. Tie them to the rack. Then come inside my office.' The deputy stepped aside to let them pass. 'Hang it all, Verne, I ain't playin' sides. But I've got a responsibility to the whole valley, not only to Three Dot or Rockin' V!'

Verne said nothing. He walked past the gaunt deputy, followed by his two men. Behind him Gallen said coldly: 'There's a lamp on my desk. Light it.'

*　　*　　*

Kip paused on the walk outside the Bonnie Bonnet. The enfolding darkness was kind to Sellout. It was like makeup on an aging woman's face; it hid the hard lines, the erosion of time, the shabbiness.

He stood on the walk, a lean, hard-muscled youngster feeling at peace with himself. His wound had healed and he had run into the man who had shot him. He was not the kind to hang onto a grudge or nurse a hate, and the physical payment he had exacted satisfied him.

The night brought coolness to the town, a relief from the burning sun. A star loomed low over the mesa. In the west the sky was still bright, a pale aquamarine, as though day were reluctant to leave.

Somewhere in the distance he heard the yipping cry of a coyote, and then in town several dogs answered. Theirs was a frantic barking, the sullen challenge of chained animals who did not know the freedom of long distances, who would not want it if it were given them. Yet somehow their barking held a vague and envious dissatisfaction.

Kip thought of what he had left behind him in San Francisco: a cold water flat, a job on the docks, in-between bouts for meager purses. It had promised him nothing. He did not have the instinct to stay in the fight game. He did not want to end up like some of the men he had seen—old and broken before their time.

He had given up nothing to come out here. And now he thought he understood a little of what his brother had meant in his letter. There was room in this land for a man to stretch his legs, to breathe.

Turning, he went up the boardwalk toward the looming bulk of the Territorial House. He walked past the corner where the deputy sheriff's office cast its pale bar of light across his path. He glanced at the three horses nosing the rack and, turning his head, saw Verne Mathis and two Three Dot riders standing by Tom Gallen's desk. Verne had a sullen look on his face. He was handing his Colt over to the deputy, and Kip felt a sudden admiration for the gaunt lawman.

Tom had a hard and thankless job. But he was working at it in the only way he knew: he was drawing Three Dot's teeth.

Kip went on into the Territorial House, where a sharp-nosed clerk accepted his money, had him sign the register, and assigned him a room and a key. 'Corner, right over the street,' he said. 'You want someone to call you in the morning?'

Kip shrugged. 'If I'm not down by six . . .' he said, and went up the creaking stairs. He found his room close with the lingering heat of the day. Crossing to the one window, he let up the shade and slid the window up. He was in darkness, looking down on the shadowy street, and he saw Verne Mathis and Tom Gallen and the Three Dot men walk by, heading for the Three Deuces.

He turned away and scraped a wood match and found the wick of the brass-based lamp on the wobbly dresser. The smoky light showed him a narrow iron bed and a chair. The only color in the room was supplied by the Navajo blanket on the bed.

A Mexican boy knocked on his door and came inside with a bucket of water which he poured into the earthenware pitcher. He looked speculatively at Kip, giggled in a high falsetto, and disappeared.

Kip grinned. He looked at himself in the dresser mirror. His face was thinner, he thought, and he liked the brownness of it. His eyes looked lighter against the tan. But his high-necked black sweater with its mended spot where Vic's bullet had torn it looked strange now. And the cap pulled over his eyes did not fit.

He was out of place here, a misfit. He was Kip Nunninger, late of San Francisco's wharfs, of Paddy's gym. He was Kid Malone, a fast man with his dukes. He looked in the mirror and wondered what it was he wanted.

He wanted to see Fred again. He wanted to see what kind of life Fred Nunninger was living in this grim, desolate land.

Somewhere out on the dark flats a train hooted a warning of its approach to the depot which shunned the town. The lonely wail lingered in the night, and it was Kip's only bond with the life he had left behind him.

He pulled off his sweater and washed his face and upper body, his eyes lingering briefly on the puckered scar on his chest. He saw that his hair was long and shaggy over his ears and neck, and he knuckled the bristle on his jaw. He could use the services of a barber.

Dressing, he went down into the lobby and asked the clerk for the whereabouts of the barbershop. He was given directions and found Leo Salito's hole-in-the-wall shop closed. He paused, teetering uncertainly on his toes.

The sound of voices and harsh laughter drifted across the street from the Three Deuces. A vague impulse took hold of him. He had been told to stick close to his room until he left. But he was a big boy, and he was not out for trouble. The devil with Tom Gallen, he thought curtly, and headed across the street.

\*       \*       \*

The Three Deuces had a high false front and a long bar and was owned by Dilly Thomas. When the railroad began building across Antelope Valley, Dilly had added a small stage

66

at the rear of the bar, knocking out the back wall and extending the room in that direction. He had imported girls and more liquor; he had expected, as did most of the town, that a boom would be on and would continue indefinitely.

For a time the entertainers he hired had brought in a lively business. The construction crews came, in to spend their pay checks, and quick-money drifters converged on Sellout. Then the rails drew away and the construction crews ceased coming to Sellout and business slacked off. The fast-buck citizens departed, like vultures from clean-picked bones. Dilly reluctantly gave up importing entertainers, and the stage fell into disuse.

Most of the entertainment in the Three Deuces now was self-made. A dozen card tables graced the walls, and an old chuck-a-luck rig stood in a corner gathering dust. Even gambling was half-hearted in Sellout. There was not enough loose money floating around to attract the professionals; most of the games were for a puncher's monthly pay.

Kip pushed through the slatted doors and stepped into the smoky room. It was a quiet night. The Rocking V men were clustered around two far tables, playing blackjack. Verne Mathis and his riders were at one corner of the long bar. Tom Gallen was at the other corner, talking to a heavy-necked, broad man of forty who was dressed a shade better than the rest of the lean, Levi-clad, gunned men at the tables.

He turned and glanced at Kip, and his shoulders straightened and his lips formed a thin curse. Then he turned back to the big man, who was scowling at Nunninger.

The youngster from Frisco walked to the bar. Verne turned as he approached and nodded without much warmth. There was a stiff wariness to the ramrod's stance; he was watching Tom and the man with the deputy sheriff.

Kip breasted the bar. 'Beer,' he told the bartender. Dilly glanced open-mouthed at Kip, wiped his mouth, and drew a glass from the keg. He set it in front of Nunninger.

One of the Rocking V poker players pushed away from the table and came to his feet. He walked toward Kip with long, quick strides. There was a heavy gun in a holster strapped to his right hip. He came up fast, and Verne, looking over Kip's shoulder, said coldly: 'Better get out of here, kid. Looks like you've got trouble headin' yore way!'

Chinook reached them before Kip turned. He put a hand on the kid's shoulder, jerked him around. He ignored Verne and the Three Dot riders, and put his long horsy face close to Kip's. 'Heard you been tellin' stories about me to the law, kid!' he snarled. 'You lookin' for trouble?'

Kip measured this man he had knocked out at the water stop on Three Dot range. This was Vic Canny's partner. He glanced briefly at the table where Vic was watching. Tom was turning away from the man at the far end of the bar.

'I settled my score with you before,' Kip murmured. He shrugged off Chinook's grip and turned to his glass of beer. He knew this was not the end of the matter, and he knew what Chinook would try to do, and he set himself for it.

The Rocking V man's fingers dug into his shoulder again, jerking him. Kip came all the way around, ducking the backhand swipe Chinook threw at his face. His left hand sank deep into the gunman's stomach, just above Chinook's belt.

The breath whooshed out of the man and he folded, his eyes rolling. Kip's crossing right tagged him on the jaw.

For a second time Chinook went back and down. He hit the floor hard and rolled over and went limp.

Tom was halfway to Kip. He stopped and turned, his Colt coming into his right hand. Vic Canny had come out of his chair. The deputy sheriff's gun froze him in a crouched position.

The man Tom had been talking to said harshly: 'What the blazes, Tom? Who is this kid?'

Tom ignored him. 'I thought I told you to stay in yore room!' he said thickly. There was anger on his tight face.

Kip's eyes held a frosty glint—'I'm twenty,' he said flatly. 'Old enough to stay out nights—'

'An' mebbe old enough to die!' Tom cut in savagely.

The heavy man moved up beside Tom, his eyes dark, watchful. 'Who is he, Tom? A Three Dot man?'

Verne Mathis said coldly: 'A friend of Three Dot, Monte. Give him trouble an' you give us trouble.'

He was taking a hand, lining the three of them with Kip, and a dangerous glint flared up in Monte Cozzens' eyes. The Rocking V men at the poker tables broke up. They were still wearing guns; they stood cold and hard, waiting for Monte's orders.

Tom Gallen's eyes had a trapped, bitter look.

'Verne, stay out of this! Get out of here! Take this fool kid with you. But get out of here!'

Verne shook his head. 'Like the kid says, we're old enough to stay out nights. If you don't want trouble, get Rockin' V out of here!'

Monte was eyeing Kip. He looked him over as though he were trying to impress Kip's looks on his mind. 'No gun,' he said wonderingly. 'Decked out like some waterfront character. Just who the devil are you, kid? What are you doing out here?'

'The name's Kip Nunninger,' Kip answered. 'And I didn't come here to start trouble. I'm heading for Yellow Horse in the morning. My brother's out there. Fred Nunninger.'

He saw Monte's eyes widen, and a strange look crossed the big man's face. There was less anger in the man now, and he had an odd, unbelieving expression. He said slowly: 'Fred Nunninger?'

Kip came alert at something in the man's tone. 'Yeah. You know my brother?'

Monte took hold of himself. He shrugged, and anger rolled back into his face. 'Heard the name somewhere. Mebbe up in Yellow Horse. Don't know him.' He glanced down at Chinook, who had rolled over on his side and was staring dazedly at the ceiling. 'What's Chinook got against you?'

Kip frowned. 'Mebbe he oughta tell you.'

Verne was tense, standing close to Kip. 'Kid,' he breathed, 'was Chinook one of the two men by the tower?'

Kip nodded. 'There's the other one—' He indicated Vic Canny. 'The redhead with the puffed lips.'

Verne turned to Tom, his voice accusing, harsh. 'You still favorin' Rockin' V?'

'I'm favorin' nobody!' Tom gritted. But he turned and eyed Monte, who was staring at Verne with a puzzled regard. 'It's been botherin' me, too, since I heard it,' he growled. 'Mebbe the kid oughta tell you about it, Monte. I want you to hear it.'

Kip told them, coldly, tersely. 'I don't know

71

why they were out there that day,' he ended. 'An' I guess I just happened to be in their way. But I don't like being shot, even if it was all a mistake.'

'I know why they were out there!' Verne cut in grimly. 'Mr Westwood got a note. It wasn't signed. But it said that if he wanted to know what had happened to his son, Brian, he should ride out at sundown to that water stop. I told him it was a trap, but he went anyway. If this kid hadn't been there, Monte's men would have killed him—'

'Whoa!' the deputy growled. 'Chinook an' Vic weren't even ridin' for Rockin' V when it happened.'

Verne said stubbornly, 'Then they were hired to do the job before—'

Monte Cozzens was surprised, or else he was a good actor. 'Just a minute, Verne!' he snapped. 'Are you accusin' me of tryin' to have Westwood killed?'

'I am!'

Cozzens took a lunging step toward the ramrod, and the Three Dot foreman squared off. Tom thrust himself between them, cocking his pistol.

'I'll shoot the first hothead who starts anythin'!' His voice was cold; it cracked sharply in the tense room.

Cozzens calmed down. He turned, and in a sudden burst of rage he reached down and hauled Chinook to his feet. He whirled the

72

sagging gunman around, jammed him against the bar. Chinook tried to twist away and grab for his gun, and Monte slapped him across the face.

Tom reached out with his gun hand and hauled Cozzens off.

Monte was breathing hard. 'All right, Chinook! Talk! This kid telling the truth?'

Hate ran its crooked finger down Chinook's long face. The marks of Monte's hands lay on his features.

'I never saw the bum before!' he snarled. 'Vic ran into him in the lunchroom. He told me some stranger was making wild talk about us. I never laid eyes on him before. But I sure expect to see him again!'

Monte took a slow breath. He turned to Vic. 'You see this kid before?'

Vic's swollen mouth twisted. 'Not until this afternoon in the lunchroom. He came up behind me an' hit me before I knew what he was up to. When the sheriff showed up, he told a wild story about me an' Chinook pluggin' him at the water tower on Three Dot W range. We weren't even in Antelope Valley then.'

Monte's rage subsided. He looked at Tom, his face hard. 'Ever stop to think that Three Dot may have hired this kid to spread that kind of story?'

Verne guffawed. 'Sure,' he clipped harshly. 'We shot the kid ourselves, then sent for Doc Spooner to patch him up so he could ride to

73

town an' tell this story; pick out two men he never saw before an' blame them for it!' His voice slurred angrily. 'Think again, Monte— think fast! You been pushin' at Three Dot. Mebbe some rustlin' to fatten yore tally, too. When Westwood wouldn't let me hit back, you start in on Cold Springs. Blast you, Monte— yo're not goin' to get away with it. Even hirin' killers—'

'That's enough from you!' Tom Gallen snapped roughly. He jerked his gun muzzle at Kip. 'Get out of here, kid! Right now!'

Kip hesitated, rebellion flickering in his eyes. But this trouble was bigger than he was. And it really didn't concern him. His trouble was with Chinook and Vic Canny; not with Monte Cozzens and the rest of Rocking V. Staying here would only invite trouble which Tom Gallen was trying desperately to avoid. He nodded.

Chinook cursed him as he walked out.

Tom turned to the Three Dot ramrod. 'You, too, Verne. Pick up yore guns at my office an' ride!'

'That an order? We bein' kicked out of town?' Verne's voice was harsh.

Tom nodded. 'For tonight. An' from now on both you an' Rockin' V check yore guns with me when you ride into town!'

Monte was scowling at Verne Mathis. His voice was thick with anger. 'I don't like yore boss, Verne. I don't like you. But I don't hire men to kill from ambush—'

'You hired Chinook an' that redheaded killer,' Verne stated flatly. 'That's enough for me.' He turned to his men. 'Finish yore drinks,' he said coldly. 'We'll ride. But we'll come back—an' we won't be checkin' our guns next time.'

They walked out, straight-backed. Tom Gallen moved away from the bar, his face slackening now, showing its tiredness. But his eyes retained a smoky, bitter look.

'I didn't figger you to be that kind, Monte,' he said thinly. 'But that kid ain't lyin'.'

'I'll kill the son—!' Chinook snarled. 'Vic an' me were never near that water stop. Mebbe somebody did shoot him. Mebbe the way he tells the story is true. Except that it wasn't me an' Vic, an' next time I see him I'm gonna kill him!'

Tom shook his head. 'He's leavin' at sunup. He better be alive an' healthy; or I'll come after you, Chinook—'

'He'll be the way you want him, Tom,' Monte said roughly. 'I promise you that.' He turned to Chinook. 'I'm takin' yore word that the kid made a mistake. But I want you to forget it, you an' Vic. An' the first man I hear of bein' caught on Three Dot range, I'll tend to myself, personally.'

He turned to the deputy. 'I don't like the Limey,' he said coldly. 'An' I'm losin' stock, too, more than I like. An' I got my reasons for

75

believin' Three Dot's behind it. When I get proof I'll show it to you. I'll expect you to back me up, Tom!'

He turned to face his riders. 'Let's get out of here.'

They tramped out, the laughter and easiness gone out of them. Tom walked to the door. He waited in the shadows while they mounted, wheeling away from the saloon rack.

He saw that Verne and his two men were still in his office. They came out and made a dark cluster on the steps, while Rocking V's hoofbeats faded in the night. Then they mounted and rode slowly out of town, taking the mesa trail to Three Dot.

Tom's shoulders sagged. He had sidetracked trouble tonight. But how long would he be able to keep the lid down on the range war which threatened? And when would Kansas strike again?

## CHAPTER SEVEN

Kip Nunninger was up with the sun. He stretched in front of the open window and looked down on the dusty width of No Water Avenue, and it struck him funny that he should be here in this shabby town in the middle of a desolate valley. Above the low building line he could see the far hills, sharp in the clear

76

morning air, remote and beckoning to him.

He took a deep breath and thought of last night's happenings and dismissed them from his mind. He felt hungry. About to turn away from the window, he saw the tall striding figure of Deputy Tom Gallen cross the street, and a smile lifted the corner of Kip's mouth.

He washed and combed his hair and was setting his cap on his head when he heard the knock on the door. He said: 'Come in, Sheriff,' and turned to appraise the lawman.

Tom Gallen was curt. He had not slept well and his arm still bothered him. He said: 'Decided to keep you company, son. For yore health.' His eyes were red-rimmed. 'I'll buy you a cup of coffee.'

Kip said: 'Thanks,' dryly, and followed Tom out into the hallway. He had no baggage. They went down and out through the deserted lobby. The sleepy desk clerk eyed them with little interest.

The early morning sun laid its red banners across the town. The morning air was cool on Kip's face.

'Sally opens up real early,' Gallen said briefly, and set out for the lunchroom.

Sally was in the kitchen when they entered. The bell brought her out to the counter. She pushed back a wisp of hair from sleepy eyes and forced a small smile to her lips. 'Coffee's warming up. Biscuits will be ready in five minutes. What are you having?'

'Just coffee for me,' the deputy said.

'All you've got,' Kip ordered, grinning. 'I'm hungry. Must be the excitement in this town. I'll take bacon, eggs, hotcakes, sausages—'

The deputy made a disgusted sound and reached for the makings. Sally said: 'I'll give you bacon and eggs and potatoes,' and disappeared into the kitchen.

Kip said: 'Hope I didn't cause you too much trouble last night, Sheriff.'

Gallen shook his head. 'None that wasn't shaping up anyway kid—' He turned as the bell jangled again, and Stumpy Peters stuck his head in the door and nodded.

Tom said: 'Come on in—I'm buyin' the coffee.' He turned to Kip, who was frowning. The bulk of a saddled horse moved against the lunchroom rack, visible through the window.

'I had Stumpy saddle yore piebald and bring it here,' Tom said. 'Save time—'

Kip's smile was a little cold. 'Want to get rid of me that bad, eh?'

'For yore own good, son,' Tom said, and turned to sip his coffee.

Sally brought out Kip's breakfast and stood by while he ate. Tom Gallen watched the youngster eat; he had another cup of coffee. He remembered when he had been fifteen years younger and had had that kind of an appetite after a night of trouble. Now he had only a dull headache and an uneasy anticipation.

He waited until Kip finished his coffee. Then he slid off the stool and jerked a thumb in a wide gesture. 'Ride out the east trail an' take the first left turn in the fork you come to. It'll take you to Yellow Horse. 'Bout fifty miles. You'll have to keep ridin' to make it by night.'

Kip stretched and smiled at the girl. 'Thanks for helpin' me out yesterday. Maybe I can do as much for you some day.'

'I hope not,' Sally answered, but there was a smile on her lips.

Kip touched his hat to her and strode off. Tom walked to the door and watched him mount the piebald; he nodded briefly at Kip's wave.

Sally said from across the room: 'Think he'll come back, Tom?'

'He'd be a fool if he did,' Gallen said shortly. 'He wouldn't last in Antelope another day—'

\*       \*       \*

All day the land seemed to lift toward the Sleepers; an empty land seared by the blazing sun, made immensely lonely by the silent and distant hills and the utter lack of movement. This was a new experience to Kip. He found himself losing the sense of time . . . he was a mote lost in a sea of sage and brush and sand. Occasionally he saw stands of scrub oak on low hills that seemed to ooze up out of the land; and once, in mid-morning, he caught a glimpse of a ranch far off against a slope. A windmill and a scatter of small gray buildings and a patch of olive green.

Shortly after noon he ran across a rusted, narrow-gauge track leading toward the Sleepers. The road he was following clung to the rails, and it gave him strange comfort; the iron road was something familiar in a land alien and remote and vaguely hostile.

The piebald was tiring. The rails began to twist and snake around crumbly cliffs; almost before he realized it he was in the broken, gullied country of the Sleepers.

The piebald snorted heavily and stopped and he let it blow, patting the sweated, dusty neck. He had stripped off his sweater, and the sun burned his back, and he knew he couldn't take too much of it. Despite the discomfort he pulled the wool over his shoulders again, feeling the skin stiff and hot on his back. He wished he hadn't been such a stubborn fool. He still had more than ninety dollars in his pocket, and a cotton shirt and a wide-brimmed hat would have been more comfortable. His eyes ached from squinting through the glare. He wiped his face with his handkerchief, feeling dust grit against his skin.

He reached for his canteen again and tilted it to his lips. He was still gulping when the last of it drained down his throat. He shook it, surprised that he was out of water; he hadn't realized how much he had drunk.

He looked around at the barren land that to his untrained eyes held no sign of life; the silence pressed down on him with a heavy, muffling hand. Uneasiness churned in him. He had not given much thought to the dryness of this country, but now, as he felt the weight of the empty canteen in his hand, his lips seemed to parch and he began to grow thirsty again. There was no sign of water, and he knew of no place where he could refill his canteen. He scanned the broken land, looking for some habitation. He caught himself then, forcing back the small voice of panic. He was acting like a real tenderfoot. He had not given thought to conserving water, and now he would have to wait until he reached Yellow Horse.

But he no longer underestimated this bare land; he knew now that a man could die out here with little commotion, ground out by impersonal and imponderable forces.

The piebald's lips were flecked with dried froth. The animal was thirsty; he had given little thought to it. Now he understood the appeal in the piebald's eyes and muttered: 'Sorry, Dusty. I'll buy you a drink soon as we get to Yellow Horse.'

It was forced humor and it left a sour taste in his mouth. He touched his heels to the animal's flanks, and the piebald moved ahead.

81

He let it pick its own pace. The piebald seemed to be searching the air for something; his nostrils quivered.

Several miles farther on he whinnied eagerly and started off the road. Kip hauled him around, but the piebald fought the bit. Finally he shrugged and let the animal have its way.

The piebald scrambled down a wash, and under a cutbank a pool of water glistened. The piebald thrust his muzzle into it, sucking water up in great gulps.

Kip's lips were as dry as wood. He slid out of the saddle and, unmindful of the piebald's closeness, buried his face in the small pool. He drank thirstily, and finally straightened and sat back. He heard a bird twitter in the brush, and he sat back and rolled himself a smoke, letting the piebald drink.

Finally the piebald turned away from the pool, shaking his head, sending drops scattering. The small bird flitted away.

The piebald began to crop at short, spiky grass that grew along the lip of the bank. Kip felt a strange peace crawl through him. He straightened and walked to the animal and took the cartridge belt out of the saddle bag.

He buckled it around his flat waist, shifting the setting of the heavy holster against his hip. He was not unfamiliar with guns; he had fired a .38 at targets before. But this walnut-handled Colt .45 was heavy in his hand. He let it slide back into the worn, slick holster and then he reached for it, fast, and fired at a rock in the wash some forty feet away.

The heavy explosion shattered the stillness. Sand spurted up two feet from the rock; the piebald jerked and snorted.

He slid the gun back into holster, and the weight of it seemed to tilt him. He tried drawing several times; his face had a red flush as he finally thrust it back into leather and unbuckled the belt. He had a lot to learn . . .

He put the gun and belt beck into his saddle bag and mounted. The piebald returned willingly to the road. The hills seemed less menacing now, and the narrow-gauge track ran ahead of him, like some old and forgotten road of his childhood.

Kip came into Yellow Horse just before dark. The place was a bitter disappointment to him: a straggle of ramshackle structures in a ravine. The rails ended at a squat abandoned structure with the sign: YELLOW HORSE, hanging askew over the open door. On the sides of the ravine were shacks, clinging stubbornly, their narrow trails grown over now.

There was a forlorn air about Yellow Horse, like an old man who had spent a boyhood dreaming and had wasted his youth away and now regretted it all. Kip rode along the darkening street, the footfalls of the piebald seeming to echo in the silence.

Yellow Horse was not entirely abandoned.

83

He saw a woman poling clothes in a wash tub in the back yard of one of the shacks off the road; somewhere in the house a child wailed disconsolately.

A saddled horse nosed the sagging rack of a two-story building midway up the street. It had been an imposing structure once. A double-decker gallery fronted it. The sign over the door read: YELLOW HORSE HOTEL.

He pulled up alongside the animal, a bay, and sat there for a moment trying to understand why his brother would be in a place like this. Or was he? It had been a year since Fred's letter . . .

He dismounted with a sinking feeling in the pit of his stomach and went up the steps and into the hotel.

There was a light on the desk, but the illumination faded out before it covered the big, dingy lobby. He sensed a flight of stairs on his right as he crossed the floor to the desk where a woman was bent over a pail wringing out a dirty mop.

She straightened as he approached, and he avoided the newly washed section of worn flooring. She loomed up taller than he, an angular Amazon past the age of repentance. Tufts of hair sprouted from her chin; her mustache was almost as thick as Kip's.

She wiped her hands in her dirty apron as he came up and eyed him with slightly veiled suspicion.

84

'Yep? What can I do for you?'

Kip said: 'I'm looking for my brother. He wrote me a letter from here. He said he was staying at the hotel in town. This would be it, wouldn't it? His name is Fred Nunninger.'

The woman stiffened. She looked past Kip into the shadows of the lobby. Someone moved back there; steps creaked softly. Kip saw the blank stare in her eyes and turned to see the man looming up on the edge of the lamplight.

He was a slim, narrow-waisted man on whose hips Colt-laden holsters seemed a natural growth. He wore a black shirt and dark pants tucked into Justin boots, and he walked with a soft careful stride, like a big cat stalking. The lamplight was reflected from dark high cheekbones.

'Lookin' for someone, amigo?' The man's voice was soft, like his walk. But that was all that was soft about him. He was older than Kip, but not much older; he looked Mexican or Indian, or some of both. His eyes were dark, like highly polished agate, and there was only one spot of color in his somber getup: the yellow silk scarf knotted on the left side of his throat.

Kip looked him over. 'I'm looking for my brother,' he said bluntly. 'Who are you?'

'Keno,' the man said. He waited, smiling, showing white teeth.

'That supposed to mean something?' Kip's

question was short.

Keno's eyes slitted, like a cat's in a sudden bright light. 'Might,' he slurred. 'Depends on who's askin', amigo!'

The woman hotel-keeper butted in. 'He's new here, Keno. He says he's Fred Nunninger's brother.'

Keno's lids came down over the sharp burst of flame in his eyes. 'Fred Nunninger, you say?' He looked at the woman, as if seeking her help. 'Hombre by that name lived here about a year ago. He had the room next to mine. He left town when the mines petered out, amigo.'

Kip's eyes showed his disappointment. 'You know where he went?' He turned to the woman. 'Did he leave any forwarding address?'

She shook her head. 'Just left.'

Keno shrugged. 'He might be anywhere, amigo. But he ain't here.'

Kip looked around the shabby, shadowed lobby. End of the line, he thought. Now what?

Keno was looking him over, his lips curled in a thin sneer. 'This is *muy malo* country, amigo. For a man without a gun—' His shoulders lifted meaningly. 'It is better you leave. Go back where you come from. That is good advice.'

Kip put his glance on the man, cold resentment stirring in him. 'I've been getting that advice since I got off the east-bound freight in Antelope Valley,' he said. 'Thanks, anyway, Keno. But I think I'll stick around awhile.'

He turned to the woman again. 'It's too long a ride back to Sellout. If you've got a room I'd like to stay here for the night.'

She looked at Keno as though waiting for his approval. Then she nodded, a dry sour woman with little kindness in her. 'If you want. There's plenty vacancies.' She reached under the counter and took a dusty register book and placed it in front of Kip. 'Sign here. That'll be a dollar four bits.'

Kip used the stub of pencil to write his name. He noticed that the date of the last registrant was more than six months old.

'Room 11,' the hotelkeeper said, pocketing Kip's silver. 'Your brother's old room. No lock on the door. Go up and make yourself at home.'

'I've got a horse outside at the rack,' Kip said levelly. 'I want him taken care of, too.'

The woman nodded. 'My husband, Jake, will see to it.' She picked up the lamp and motioned toward the dark staircase. 'I will show you the way—'

They left Keno standing by the desk, a dark, lean figure holding his silence. The smoky lamp cast its light over scrubbed wooden stairs that creaked underfoot. At the head of the narrow hallway she stopped before a door on the panels of which a number 11 was painted in dark green.

'There's a light on the table by the bed,' she said. 'We serve supper in the dining room downstairs in an hour.'

Her shadow was long and distorted behind her as she left him.

*       *       *

Kip turned to the door with an empty, dragged-out feeling. Fred was gone. It was not entirely unexpected; deep inside him he had sensed that he might be chasing a will-o'-the-wisp. Still, Fred's last letter had sounded optimistic, as though he had come upon something which he expected to pay off.

Kip opened the door to a small, cramped corner room where he could look through the window on the street. The gulch wall limited his view of the sky. He felt closed in, and the sense of futility depressed him.

These were the Sleepers, he thought dismally; these were the hills he had viewed so expectantly from Brent Westwood's veranda. And this was Yellow Horse, a dying town clinging stubbornly to some impossible hope.

Movement on the walk directly below him caught his attention. An old, bent figure was untying the piebald. He turned and led the animal to the alley between the hotel and the untenanted, sagging structure on the left and disappeared.

A cigaret butt made a red streak through the night as someone on the porch discarded it. It hit the dust in the middle of the street and died in a shower of sparks. A shadow moved into Kip's line of vision and mounted the bay, and Kip saw that it was the gunman called Keno.

The bay wheeled away from the rack and went up the narrow street and faded into the darkness.

Kip frowned. He pulled the shade down and found the lamp and lighted it. The room was similar to that which he had occupied in the Territorial House last night; it had the same dismal, impersonal quality.

He sat on the bed and ran his fingers through his hair, trying to pull the pattern of his next move into focus. He didn't want to go back to San Francisco. Perhaps he could get a job with Westwood. There wasn't much he could do, but he was willing to learn.

Someone knocked on the door. He said: 'Sure—come on in—' and watched an oldish, white-haired man come into the room. The man had thick, bowed shoulders, horny hands. He dragged his right leg as he walked, but his bright blue eyes had a searching quality.

He said: 'I'm Jake Horner. My wife Abigail says to tell you supper is being put on the table downstairs. If you want chow, come an' git it.' He paused, grinned with real humor. 'Ain't no other place to eat in town, anyhow.'

Kip said: 'I'll be right down, Jake.' The man started to turn away, and Kip got up and called: 'Jake! You been in Yellow Horse long?'

'Since the first strike, ten years ago.' Jake moved his quid of tobacco into his other cheek, swelling it as though he had suddenly developed a toothache. 'Seen it rich, seen it poor. Useta be seven thousand people in this gulch. Strung out all over, they was—tents, soddies, shacks. Place never slept. Sanny Fe run a spur in here an' sucked out all the gold ... It's dead now, fella. An' it ain't ever gonna get alive again.'

Kip caught the underlying sadness in the man's tone. 'I'm Fred Nunninger's brother,' he said. 'Fred wrote to me from here a year ago. Did you know him?'

'Fred?' Jake's brows knitted and he looked away from Kip. 'He know you were coming?'

Kip shook his head. 'I wanted to surprise him. I got tired of San Francisco—'

Jake sucked his lips in over his stubby teeth. He looked around for a place to spit and found the cobwebby can in the corner. He mumbled, not looking at Kip, 'Don't rightly know what to tell you, son. But you can ask Kansas about Fred!'

'Kansas?' Kip's voice was stiff. 'The outlaw?'

Jake's eyes held a wary gleam as he backed to the door. 'Reckon that's what he is, son. You ask him. Mebbe he'll tell you about yore brother—'

He turned and closed the door on Kip, and the sound of his shuffling descent faded into the stillness.

\* \* \*

A half-dozen stubborn, out-at-the-elbows miners sat around the big round dining table in the hotel dining room. Kip joined them. They were whiskered, ragged, weathered men who clung to the hope that another ten feet of digging in their shafts would bring them to a rich vein of gold. They were the men who couldn't believe that Yellow Horse was dead; that all the gold had been picked clean. They were the men who lived in the past and with the ghosts of the past.

They didn't even see Kip. They talked of drift and assay, of shoring and drainage; the talk meant nothing to Kip. And they were tired men. They left the table at the end of the meal and went upstairs to bed. Abigail went back to the kitchen. Jake disappeared. Kip wanted to talk to Jake again, but the old man was not to be found.

He wandered out through the lobby and paused on the sagging veranda.

Somewhere in the darkness an accordion made music; the gay lilt of its melody only emphasized the squalor of the dying town. He stepped off the veranda, wanting to get away from this hotel where his brother had lived, and to which he had come with high hopes. The thought of going up to his room depressed him.

He walked down the dusty street toward the music and found that it came from inside a squat, one-story tar-papered shack near the south end of town.

He looked in over the slatted doors. A half-dozen men stood at the bar, watching a dark, fleshy Mexican girl dance in the middle of the small room. Kerosene lamps smoked, mingling with the thick cigaret and cigar smoke that made a haze in the room.

Kip went inside. The men at the bar turned to look at him. They didn't look like miners, or town men, either. They were hard men, wearing belt guns. The sad-faced accordionist let his fingers slide along the keyboard and drop off . . . the girl stopped dancing.

Kip walked to the bar. The bar tender waved a thick arm to the musician and the Mexican shrugged. He picked up the tune again, and this time another Mexican girl came out of a doorway behind him to join the girl in the middle of the room. She was younger and slimmer than the first one and might have been her daughter. They danced.

The men clapped and hoorahed, and a brawny fellow drew his Colt and fired into the ceiling. Two of the men left the bar, taking the bottle with them; they scooped the girls up under one arm and headed for the side door. The accordionist kept playing, his face dark and impassive.

Kip felt a vast disgust. There was a meanness about the place, an air of obscene decadence, like a fine wine allowed to age too long and which had gone sour.

He turned to leave, and the one-eyed, burly bar tender said: 'Hey, Mac! What you drinkin'!'

The others remaining at the bar turned to look at him. He saw flat amusement glint in the pale gray eyes of the man nearest him—a rangy, hard-jawed man with a broken nose.

'Give him sassyparilla, Zeke,' the man growled. 'You kin see the kid ain't been weaned yet.'

Kip said: 'I changed my mind,' and moved away, not wanting to get into trouble.

He was almost to the door when a loud explosion rocked the room and the board flooring an inch from his right toe splintered. He stopped. The rangy man had a smoking Colt in his fist. 'It's not polite to refuse a drink, kid,' he said. 'Zeke's got yore sassyparilla for yuh.'

The one-eyed bar tender was uncorking a bottle. Kip hesitated. The men at the bar were just liquored up enough to shoot first and then think of consequences. And, he thought bleakly, who would make anything of it? Sheriff Tom Gallen, down in Sellout? Well, he'd been warned that this was rough country, hadn't he?

He turned and went back to the bar and picked up the bottle of sarsaparilla. 'To you,' he said to the rangy man with the Colt, and drank it.

The others edged around, grinning. One of them said: 'Stranger, in town, eh? Don't look like a railroad dick, but you might be. You a railroad dick?'

Kip shook his head.

'Might be one of them Pinkerton hawkshaws,' another guffawed. 'Heard tell they are real cool hombres—'

'You out after the reward for Kansas, kid? Must be a big one by now. Kansas' been holdin' up too many trains in this section, ain't he? Heard he robbed the bank in Sellout the other day. You know about it?'

Kip remained silent. They were drunk and there was meanness in them. He began to feel his helplessness, and he didn't like it. Even a small man was big behind the muzzle of a gun.

'They won't never get Kansas,' an oldish, whiskered man said. 'He's too smart. An' some day he'll sit right under their noses, a big, respectable citizen—'

The rangy man jabbed a hard elbow into the man's stomach. 'You talk too much, Sam. Specially with a skinful of Zeke's rotgut in yuh!' He turned a hard face to Kip. 'This is a private party, kid. You had yore drink. Now get out!'

Kip nodded. He felt his neck burn, but he held the swift rise of anger. He had been treated like some harmless boy, and he was. If he had made a move, he would have been killed.

He walked back along the dark street, trying to remember his brother; wondering how Fred Nunninger, also a product of San Francisco's docks, had adapted himself to this life. Fred had a driving, callous force about him. He would be somebody if it killed him. Kip wondered if Fred was dead.

'Ask Kansas,' Jake had said. But how was he to ask Kansas?

He walked back to the darkened lobby and climbed the stairs to his room. He closed the door and stood in the darkness; the wail of the accordion reached him through the night, lost and sad. He felt depressed.

He had come as far as he could, and now there was no further point in looking. He kicked off his shoes and tossed his hat on the chair. He lay on the bed and heard one of the girls laugh shrilly. After a while he fell asleep.


## CHAPTER EIGHT

The man named Keno rode through the night on a dark and twisted trail. He rode where there was no trail; splashed across a small

95

stream brawling over stones, and came at length to a small valley almost directly behind the gulch where Yellow Horse straggled in shabby isolation. Although there was a shorter way to town, Keno came this way because it was one of the rules laid down by Kansas.

A man challenged him from the darkness, and he gave the password and rode on. The light in the cabin was like a yellow eye, probing the darkness. He rode up to it and ground-reined the bay and entered the cabin without knocking.

Four men were playing poker around a small homemade table. He closed the door, and Sol Mako, half Oriental, lifted a bland face from his poker hand and grunted: 'Howdy, Keno. How'd you make out in town?'

Keno ignored the question. He asked one of his own. 'Me boss back?'

Mako jerked his head. 'In there. With the stooge.'

Keno started for the rear door. Mako's voice held a sour warning. 'You know how he is, Keno. He's talkin' business—'

'He'll listen to me,' Keno said roughly, and knocked on the door.

There was a stir in the room behind the door boards. Then a man's hard, irritated voice grated: 'Who is it?' Keno opened the door. He closed it and put his back against it, meeting the angry stare of the man standing by the small window. He was a short man, not

96

more than five seven. But he had wide shoulders which bulged against his rust-brown coat and he wore pearl-handled Colts in twin holsters. He had a thick waist, flat and hard as a washboard, and the beginnings of jowls. But there was nevertheless a catlike quality in this man; the same smooth working of muscles, of balance, that there was in Keno.

'I'm busy!' Kansas snapped. 'Wait outside.'

Keno put his regard on the older, paunchy man at the table. There was a quart of Bourbon on the table at the man's elbow, and Keno knew that Kansas didn't drink.

Judge Silas Weller had been a barker in a sideshow, a not-so-good Shakespearian player, a con man, a buffoon. He had never been a lawyer. But he could look the part and he could roll his words with sonorous authority. He was the prop for Kansas' plan of conquest in Antelope Valley; the perfect front man.

Keno knew this about Weller.

He put his attention on Kansas, reading the danger signals in the outlaw boss' eyes. 'You'll want to hear what I have to say,' he said thinly. Keno was the only man in Kansas outlaw bunch who was not afraid of him. 'But if you think I should wait—'

'Spill it!' Kansas snapped. 'You didn't leave town tonight just for the night air.'

Keno nodded. '*Si*—I have news. A stranger has come to Yellow Horse; a kid who wears a strange hat and a sweater that comes up

97

around his neck. No guns. He says his name is Kip Nunninger and he's looking for his brother—'

A surprised cry broke from Kansas. He came away from the window, his eyes narrowing incredulously. 'Keno! The kid?'

Keno shrugged. 'He's stayin' at Abigail's place, in yore old room. We told him you had left Yellow Horse. You left no forwarding address. He took it pretty hard—'

Kansas lifted his hands, then dropped them in a futile gesture. 'The darn fool—'

'He's ridin' a Three Dot W hoss, Kansas. A piebald.' Keno's teeth reflected the lamplight. 'I thought you'd like to know.'

Fred Nunninger, alias Kansas, nodded. 'He should have waited,' he muttered; he was now talking to himself. 'Another four, five months . . . then I'd have written to him.'

He turned sharply, his glance spearing Judge Weller. 'Wait here!' he commanded harshly. 'I'll be back. We'll go over details then.'

He picked his hat from a wall hook and turned to Keno. 'We'll pay my brother a visit, Keno.'

He was thinking of the plans he had for Kip. The boy's coming was premature and unwelcome. Fred was playing a grim game here, and there was no place in it for a green kid. This was rough country. It wasn't like fighting for a few lousy bucks in a makeshift ring in a dive on Market Street. A man used a gun out here, not his fists. And he learned to use it well—or he died!

Kip was awakened by a heavy hand shaking him. He tried to sit up and the hand shoved him back. He saw the dark shape of the man looming over him, and starlight, coming in through the window, glinted from the muzzle of a Colt held less than two inches from his nose.

A voice, distorted and muffled through the folds of a cotton handkerchief, ordered: 'On yore feet, sonny. Don't make any noise. Don't try anything!'

The pressure on his chest eased, and Kip sat up. He could see a half-dozen figures in the room. There was enough light to show him they were masked by handkerchiefs. Gunned men. He thought he recognized one or two of them as the men he had run into in the saloon at the south edge of town.

He said angrily: 'All right. I got ninety dollars in my pocket. Take it and leave me alone—'

The man who had awakened him laughed shortly. 'Ninety dollars ain't enough, kid. We want you.'

Kip was wide awake now. Anger crawled through him, fretting against the barrier of caution.

'Get yore hat an' yore boots on,' the man said, 'an' take whatever else yuh got. You ain't comin' back.'

Kip swung his legs over the bed. He found his shoes and got into them, and his voice was thin. 'Like fun I ain't. I got business here. I want to see a man named Kansas!'

There was a strange silence in the room, as though he had said the wrong thing. Then the short man shoved him, hard. His voice was heavy. 'Get movin', kid—'

The rough hand drove caution from Kip. He spun around, driving his right into the short man's face. The man fell back and he crowded him, using his left. The man's knees buckled and he cursed, and then lights exploded in Kip's head and he fell forward. The short man clubbed him under the ear as he fell.

He didn't feel the hard floor. The lights wheeled around in his head and pain was a sharp, thrusting knife behind his eyes. He felt himself lifted and dropped across the bed. He couldn't move, though he wanted to.

He heard the short man's voice again, mixed with cursing. '. . . said not to hurt him . . .' Then he felt hands on him, and he was lifted and held between two men.

His feet dragged as they took him out of the room. They went down into the lobby, and if any of the other occupants of the hotel had heard the commotion they were being quiet about it.

Horses were bunched at the dark rail. Someone had saddled and taken Kip's piebald around to join them. Kip was lifted up into the saddle. He sagged over the horn and clung to it, fighting the nausea in his stomach. The pain behind his eyes made him squint.

They rode away, out of the dying gold camp. Someone led Kip's piebald. They rode in silence, only the creaking of leather and the sound of iron-shod hoofs breaking the eternal stillness.

After a while Kip straightened in the saddle. The nausea had subsided and only the pain remained. He glanced at the riders flanking him, hard, masked men. He wondered what they wanted of him. It wasn't robbery, for they had not taken his money.

They seemed to ride a long time. Finally he heard a train whistle from afar, wailing like a lost and hunted animal in the night.

They rode down a long slant of ground and hit a graveled grade. The rails gleamed in the starlight, leading into the blackness of the night. Way off to Kip's left as he sat saddle on the restive piebald, he saw a yellow light search the darkness.

The train whistle sounded again, asking its question of the night.

The short man said: 'Get off that cayuse, kid. This is where we say *adios*.'

Kip eyed the silent riders. The train was beginning to climb the grade toward them, a good two miles away. Its heavy puffing reached them.

101

'We're givin' yuh a free ride back to where you came from,' the short man said. 'Get wise. Don't come back!'

Kip's anger broke loose. His voice was sharp. 'Who in blazes are you?'

'Name's Kansas,' the short man said. 'I boss this country, kid.' He waved a hand in a wide sweep to indicate what he meant, and Kip saw the flash of the man's ring. He edged the piebald close and leaned over for a closer look. Kansas' hand was resting lightly on his pommel. The ring had a coiled snake design in gold with a small red ruby for an eye.

The ring had belonged to his brother!

'Kansas?' Kip's voice was thick. 'That ring belonged to my brother. Where is he?'

'Who?' There was a cold, ominous ring to the short man's voice.

'Fred Nunninger.'

Kansas chuckled. 'Fred's dead. I killed him myself—'

Kip hit him. The blow spilled the man out of the saddle, and Kip swung his leg over the horn and tried to follow.

A gun exploded heavily in the night and the bullet clipped a swatch of wool from Kip's shoulder. Then another Colt slammed against the silence, and the rider spurring toward Kip with uplifted gun jerked in the saddle, and his gun arm dropped limply.

Kansas put his shoulder against his horse and shoved the animal aside. He faced Kip, his

102

Colt smoking. He dropped the gun into his holster and reached up and pulled the youngster out of the piebald's saddle.

'Teach you a lesson, sonny,' he said thickly.

Kip's head ached. He tried to reach the man and found him gone; then a hard fist sank into his kidney. He stumbled, and the outlaw boss hit him again, jolting blows that spun Kip around, mashed his lips, dropped him.

Kansas reached down and dragged Kip erect and hit him again. Punishing blows. Face and stomach and kidneys. And when he stepped back Kip lay on the gravel skirt, a limp, unconscious figure.

They dragged him away from the rails. The light from the engine was spearing up the track. They waited in the shadows until the engine loomed up, crawling on the grade. Then the man on Kansas' left fired a shot through the cab.

'*Hold it!*'

The frightened engineer hauled back on the brake lever. The long freight ground to a halt, shuddering down its length.

A brakeman came running along the tops of the cars. A shot at his feet stopped him and drove all further curiosity from him.

They searched the box cars until they found an empty. Kansas bent over Kip, thrust a thick roll of bills into Kip's trouser pocket. Then they dumped him into the car, slid the door shut.

They rode back to the engine panting like some tired mammoth on the grade. 'Roll it!' Kansas ordered grimly.

The engineer fed steam to the drive wheels. They spun on the iron, driving sparks up into the night. They slowed. Slowly the train began to move; couplings clashed like tortured souls. It rolled on, heading west.

Kansas took the handkerchief from his face then. There was a cut on his lip and a mouse growing over his left eye. The man he had shot, Sawyer, was bent over his saddle horn, his eyes sullen.

The outlaw boss waited until the red and green lights of the caboose flickered out behind a curve. He thought of his kid brother in the boxcar; of the boy he had raised. It seemed a long time ago and another life.

'Let's ride,' he growled. 'That's all for tonight!'

He mounted and rode alongside the wounded man. 'I told you I didn't want the kid hurt, Sawyer. Next time you disobey an order, I won't shoot for yore arm.'

They rode into the shadows and the hills of the Sleepers.

\*     \*     \*

The clacking click of a flat wheel penetrated Kip's head. He stirred, and a groan broke involuntarily through his cut lips. He felt the

104

hard floor under him and the jolting of the train, and consciousness came back in a rush. But he lay on his back, looking up into the blackness. He knew he was in a boxcar and that the train was moving.

His face felt stiff, and he touched it. There was blood on his chin, already dried. He licked his cut lips tentatively, exploring the cut inside his cheek with his tongue. His ribs ached and his eyes hurt from the pain in his head.

After a while he sat up. He found he could move, although the pain in his head grew intense with movement. So he lay still and let his mind work on what had happened, and the hate inside him began small and tight and moved up until it tasted like bile in his mouth.

'Shoved around, beat up and shipped home,' he muttered. 'Kid Malone, pride of the waterfront.' A burning shame stung him. He got to his feet and walked to the door and slid it open and watched the night-darkened rangeland slide by. The train was moving at a moderate pace, but by morning, he knew, he could be miles out of this country.

And he didn't want to leave.

Standing there, fighting the weakness in his legs, he felt the bulge against his thigh. He put his hand in his pocket and his fingers closed over the roll of bills. He took them out, wondering. Even in the dim starlight he could see that he had several hundred dollars in his fist.

*Why?*

Beat up, dumped into a west-bound freight, warned to get out of the country and stay out. And yet someone had put this money in his pocket. Someone had shown him uncalled for kindness.

It didn't make sense.

His breath sighed between his teeth. His eyes searched the night, and then he saw the far away yellow glow in the darkness. And then it was gone and only the darkness remained.

But out there was a house of some sort.

He took the chance. He jumped with the forward motion of the train. He landed on his feet beside the gravel skirt and spilled forward. He skinned his shins and knees and the palms of his hands, and the pain in his head drove a sharp spike between his eyes.

But beyond that he was unhurt. He pulled himself to his feet and watched the caboose click by, flicking its lights at him. Then he turned and headed in the direction of the light he had seen.

He walked what seemed to him a long long time. False dawn was lightening the sky in the east. He must have missed it, he thought grimly. And then he heard a horse snort heavily in the shadows ahead.

And a voice called out, too high-pitched to be a man's yet with a man's harsh timbre: 'That's far enough. Yore on Havison land now, fella.'

# CHAPTER NINE

Malvina Havison tossed on her bed in the darkness of her room. She was restless; she often had these spells of sleeplessness. She had read until her eyes ached and then she had gone to bed. But she lay wide-eyed, hearing the stillness of the night.

Finally she jerked her covers away and dressed. She was a big woman, bony and hard-fleshed. She stood five feet eight in her stocking feet. But there was a certain grace in her movements, an athletic carriage of body. Her hands were big, hard-palmed, rough. At thirty the wheat-colored down on her cheek was noticeable at close quarters.

She was not pretty. There was plainness in the broad, crudely fashioned features, the too big nose. Her eyes were blue and level in appraisal, and her hair was the color of the down on her face.

Her sisters slept in the other room: Meg, prettiest and youngest; and Nora, five years older than Malvina. Prim, homely Nora with the Havison big nose and big hands and without the Havison recklessness or passion. Nora slept the peaceful sleep of one without impossible yearnings and ambitions. Gentle Nora. She slept well.

Malvina was dressed now, and habit made

107

her turn to the window for a look at the darkened rangeland. She heard a train whistle in the loneliness of early morning, and something inside her responded and cried out at the trap her life had become. She wanted to leave this rickety old house where she had been born thirty years ago this summer. She wanted to leave forever this house of lonely, forgotten women.

She heard Meg moan in her sleep, and pain was a cleansing knife in her, cutting away the rebellion in her soul. Meg had been hurt, too. But she had won her escape. Only at night was Meg not free. Only at night, in the dark and in her subconscious thoughts, did the inferno she had escaped from break through to torment her.

Malvina moved quickly out of the room and down the stairs, her steps creaking on old floor boards and reminding her of all the haunted houses she'd read about. She was glad to escape the house. She stepped out into the cool night and the starshine touched her face. It softened and transformed the plainness and the hardness.

Vanity whinnied softly and came to her, nosing her through the pole bars of the small corral. Malvina had named the dusty mare thus—the horse was trim and beautiful, as Malvina knew she herself was not. She let Vanity out, and the mare followed her to the shed where she found bridle and saddle without need of light. She had done this time and again in the months since he had quit coming . . .

Vanity whickered eagerly, and Malvina said: 'Shh-h-h-h!' thinking of her sisters. But they never wakened.

She rode out into the night, out of the cup in the low hills which held the slowly disintegrating buildings of Broken Quirt. Broken Hopes would have been more apt, she thought bitterly.

She had loved her father, despite his shortcomings and his weaknesses. Gunner Havison had been everywhere, and to hear him talk he had done everything. He had a largeness about him that overshadowed his lies and his weakness for whiskey.

Gunner Havison had come to Antelope Valley when deer moved in herds across it; when the Pawnees, wintering west of their usual haunts, camped on the banks of Devil's Creek.

Gunner Havison and John Straw had pioneered this valley. It had been theirs and they had had large dreams, dreams bigger than either of them. John Straw had wound up with a stable in the town of Sellout, and Gunner Havison had left behind him memories and Broken Quirt, a down-at-the-heels spread run by his three spinster daughters.

She heard a chicken cluck sleepily, and Cerebrus, the old tan and white hound, came trotting out of the night to investigate. He was too old to bark; he waited, tail wagging, for the command she always gave him.

'Go on; go back to sleep!' He wagged his tail harder and turned back to the shadows of the barn.

Malvina rode out of the yard and took the path toward the creek. On the rise overlooking the small trickle over the white sand bed were the crosses marking the graves of her mother and father and her infant brother—the one who had died before he had reached his first year.

Way over to the left, and close to the overhang, was another mound. There was no headboard over it, but a yellow-painted tomato can held freshly cut zinnias.

She wheeled Vanity away, spurring the startled mare. The animal broke into a gallop, and Malvina let her have her head. They headed for the tracks, and in the distance now she heard the rumble of the approaching train, and topping a rise she saw the engine's beam probing the night.

The west-bound freight. Its metallic rattle sounded clear in the early morning stillness. She pulled the mare to a stop, and settled back, her body tense with the pull of her thoughts. They rode with that train toward the coast, toward all the far places she had never seen . . . away from this valley and this narrow, stifling life she led. The voice of rebellion cried inside her, beating with its fists against the barrier erected by duty to her sisters. It spent itself finally and left her drained and without hope.

She slumped in the saddle, and Vanity moved restlessly. It was time for another run in the cool, clean air just before dawn. But Malvina lay slumped and unheeding.

The train was gone now, lost in the rising upland shadows. The mare stood still, ears pricked for the sound of someone approaching. Even Malvina heard it; she straightened slowly. She wore a belt gun, a Smith & Wesson .38. It was part of her dress, as much her attire as the old cotton shirt and faded Levis.

The figure loomed up out of the night, and Dusty snorted.

She said harshly, drawing the .38: 'That's far enough. You're on Havison land now, fella.'

Kip stopped. He could make out the shape of a woman on a trim mare; she loomed up behind the muzzle of a gun, A woman in a man's shirt and man's pants; there was a man's directness in her voice.

'Don't mean any harm, ma'am,' he said. 'I'm lost. Looking for a place to rest up till daylight.'

She peered down at him, her eyes hard and distrustful. 'What happened to your face, boy?'

He stiffened at her use of the word 'boy.' 'I had an argument with a gun boss named Kansas. I came out second best.'

'Kansas?'

He caught her inflection of startled surprise. And something more; something he couldn't define. But there was knowledge of the outlaw boss in her tone, and he answered grimly: 'Yeah. He killed my brother!'

The shadowy figure on the mare sat still. In that moment she seemed to draw away from him. Finally she whispered: 'Who is your brother?'

'Fred Nunninger,' he replied coldly. 'My name's Kip Nunninger.'

She sighed. It was a strange sound in the quiet. Then she said briskly: 'You look beat, Kip. Climb aboard. Vanity can take us both back to Broken Quirt.'

He nodded his thanks. 'I sure appreciate it, ma'am—'

'It's Miss Havison,' she said, and her voice held a kindly note. 'Miss Malvina Havison. I run Broken Quirt.'

He looked up at her. 'Did you know my brother?'

She hesitated. 'Yes.' Her voice was a whisper; it implied more than she said. 'But not too well, it seems . . .'

She slipped her left foot out of the stirrup, and he climbed up behind her. They rode in silence. He was too sore and too tired to pay much attention to the lightening countryside. But he remembered it when they splashed through a shallow trickle of water and the outbuildings of Broken Quirt came into view, ghostly in the morning grayness.

The light in the ranchhouse window shone weakly. It was in the kitchen and it burned all night; sometimes Meg Havison woke up screaming and came down into the kitchen, and the light comforted and calmed her.

They rode into the yard, and Cerebrus came to greet them, sniffing at Kip's legs when he dismounted.

Malvina said: 'My sisters are still asleep. They help me run the ranch.' She led the mare to the corral, where she unsaddled Vanity and turned her loose.

A thin, stoop-shouldered wraith met them at the door. Nora Havison was as tall as Malvina, but slat-thin and with features like old china on which the lines of age had made tiny cracks. Her nose hooked over her mouth and almost met her chin, but her eyes had a soft brown, kindly look. She nodded her head, although no one had spoken, it was a habit of acquiescence she had developed as a child and never lost.

Malvina said: 'Look, Nora. We've got a man in the house—at last!' There was a harsh irony to her voice; and a cruel baiting. 'See if you can't prepare him a man-sized breakfast, like you used to make for Paw.'

Nora bobbed her head. 'Shh-h-h—' She put fingers to her lips. 'Meg is still sleeping.' She looked shyly at Kip.

'He's had some trouble,' Malvina said curtly. 'But we won't bother him with a lot of fussing, will we, Nora? He'll be staying with us for a while.' She turned to Kip. 'You can rest here, Kip.'

He tried a smile on his swollen lips. 'If it's no bother, ma'am—I mean Miss Havison.'

She shook her head. 'No bother at all. And if you have no other place to go, we could use a man around the ranch for a few weeks. There are many things that need doing.'

He looked at her. He could see her clearly now in the light of the kitchen lamp. Behind her, through the kitchen window, the eastern sky was flushing a pale pink. He saw her standing big and competent-looking. She did not strike him as a woman who needed a man around. Yet there was a softness around her mouth, and her eyes held an expression of pleasure, as though she were pleased with some secret she alone knew.

He thought over his predicament. He had ninety-seven dollars, plus the money Kansas had put in his pocket; money he did not intend using. He was not hard up. But he needed some place where he could think until he was ready to settle his score with Kansas.

He had no illusions as to his ability to do this at the moment. Kansas himself had told him that a man didn't settle things with his fists in this country.

He thought of Three Dot W, and Westwood,

and Westwood's offer of a job. But he hesitated to get Three Dot involved in his troubles. He had had his run-in with Rocking V; and with a range war already threatening, his being with Three Dot wouldn't help things.

So he nodded to Malvina, wondering what was behind this hard-eyed woman's offer. It didn't make sense. He was a complete stranger here, and from what he had heard the Havison women were not friendly.

Malvina Havison rubbed her hands briskly, like a man who had just concluded a favorable deal. 'Good. We can't pay you much. But you'll have a place to sleep, and we'll feed you well. And you can stay as long as you like.'

'I might stay longer than you'll want me to,' he said. He fingered his jaw. 'I'm new to this country. I've had a lesson pounded home to me. A man isn't any good out here unless he can handle a gun. I aim to spend my spare time learning how.'

Malvina's eyes glittered. 'That's your affair, of course. I have my father's gun, a Colt Peacemaker. You can have it and all the ammunition you need, in return for the chores you'll be asked to do.'

'Good enough,' he agreed. He turned and wrinkled his nose at the breakfast dish Nora brought in to the table by the window. Eggs on thick slices of steak. And biscuits, warm and fluffy. The pungent odor of coffee filled the kitchen; turning to look at this frail Havison

115

woman, he felt an odd sense of familiarity, akin to the barely remembered peace of his mother's kitchen . . .

Nora smiled shyly. 'Nice to have a man in the house. Won't Meg be surprised?' She caught her breath then, as though she had said a naughty word, and looked at her sister. Her hand came up to her mouth, and she backed away and left the room.

Malvina said with harsh indifference: 'Nora's an old maid by choice,' leaving the implications of that remark to get across to Kip. She sat down across from him and poured herself coffee.

'Go ahead—eat,' she directed. 'I like to see a man eat breakfast.'

She talked as he ate.

'I was born on this spread, in this house,' she said. 'I helped Paw fight off Indians in the summer of sixty-one. My mother is dead and buried on the hill overlooking Devil's Creek. She's been dead all of twenty years.' She sipped her coffee. Her voice was dry and matter of fact, as though she were recounting a story she had heard. 'My father was a man who dreamed big. He was a mountain man tamed by a wife and his children. He settled here when the valley belonged to the antelope. He needed boys to help him with his dream of building the biggest ranch in the Territory—he had three girls instead. My brother was the last to be born, and he died before he was a year

116

old.

'My father was a weak man, Kip. Oh, he was big and strong. He once killed a bear with a club and knife, in the Sleepers. But he was weak where it counts. He couldn't stand disappointment. When he received a setback he wanted to leave, get away from it. The year the big blizzard wiped us out finished him. He started drinking hard . . . he was always a drinking man. He let the ranch go to pieces. Some of the land he sold for taxes, some just to eat. And finally he was killed; knifed while he was drunk, for what he had in his pockets.

'I've been running Broken Quirt since then.' Her lips curled in a brittle sneer. 'My father called this ranch Quirt; I changed it to Broken Quirt. He called it Quirt because with it he was going to whip the valley. I have no such illusions.' She smiled at him over her coffee cup. 'I read too much, Kip. That's the only fun I have, reading. Don't take it up. It makes one restless and unhappy. It makes one look for something and want something one cannot get . . .'

Kip made no comment. A strange woman, he thought. Big and masculine-looking in pants and shirt—and yet there was a woman's softness and a woman's yearning behind that hard exterior.

The light grew stronger in the kitchen, making the lamplight dingy and useless. A bird hopped to the window sill and chirped his

117

greeting, cocking his head to one side and eyeing them with bright interest. Then something else caught his attention and he flew off.

Kip finished his breakfast. He settled back, his bruises hurting him now and reminding him of the night. He moved his shoulders in a fighter's gesture and tried to work out the stiffness; he wanted to shake off the tiredness settling like a weight over him. 'If you'll show me what you want done—'

'No hurry,' Malvina said. 'You need sleep. I'll show you where you'll bunk. There's a room in the barn where Paw was going to have his office. He built the partition when he still had his dreams . . .'

Kip nodded. He was too tired to argue. He got to his feet and was aware that someone had come down from the upstairs bedrooms and was coming into the kitchen. He turned, and his glance lighted up as he saw a young blond girl pause, in the doorway. She had a stiff prettiness, like that of a young girl, and her voice was light and childish as she said: 'Malvina, I heard someone here—'

Then her eyes fell on Kip and her reactions were unaccountable to Kip. She went stiff, as though a knife had been thrust through her body. Her eyes widened and rolled and the whites showed. Her hands clenched. She gasped: 'Brian . . .' and her knees buckled under her and she started to fall.

Kip caught her before she hit the floor. He reached her a split-second before Malvina; she lay in his arms. He looked questioningly at the older woman.

'I'll take her,' Malvina said roughly. She took the girl from Kip's arms and held her as easily as Kip had. She turned and walked up the stairs with her.

Kip waited in the hallway, frowning. He heard a cautious step behind him and turned to see Nora wringing her hands. 'I knew,' she whispered. 'I knew that Meg would think it was him . . .'

Malvina came back down to join them. Her face was wooden. 'That's Meg,' she said. 'She's not well. I think you frightened her.'

'I'm sorry—' Kip started to say. But she brushed his apology aside.

'You didn't do anything, Kip. But Meg's suffered a shock. She used to be in love with Brent Westwood's boy, Brian. Westwood, in case you don't know, owns the big ranch to the west, the Three Dot W. Brian disappeared some time ago under strange circumstances. Meg is a spoiled child. She always got what she wanted from Paw. She wanted Brian. When he disappeared, something happened to her. Now every young man reminds her of Brian.'

Kip nodded. 'I'm sorry I frightened her,' he said.

'She'll get used to you,' Malvina said. 'She sits by the window a lot, in the rocking chair.

119

She likes to read, too. She doesn't talk much any more. But if she should talk to you sometime, and it doesn't make sense, you'll understand.'

He nodded. 'I think I will.'

'Come,' she said. She led the way out of the house. Daylight showed him the pitiful attempts to keep the ranch going. There were flowers around the sagging house. A small fence had been whitewashed. But the barn needed paint badly and the corral was in need of repair.

He said: 'I'm better at cutting fish or sailing a yawl, Miss Havison. Or,' he held up a cocked right fist, 'using this to earn a living. I've never worked on a ranch before. But I'll learn. I promise you that.'

She smiled without humor. 'I'm sure of it.'

They went into the barn, and she opened a rough plank door in a boarded-off section. The room was about eight by ten feet. There was a cobwebby window that let in a dirt-filtered light. There was a closeness in the stale air that hit Kip at once. Except for the wooden bunk with straw ticking and a chair and a wooden desk built against the inner wall, the room was bare.

'I'll get you some blankets,' Malvina said, and left him.

Kip sat on the bunk. He thought over what had happened to him. The night's events were blurred, distorted by a growing weariness. He lay back on the ticking and closed his eyes.

He was asleep when Malvina came into the room. She looked down at him, and pity glistened in her eyes. She drew the blanket over his sprawled figure.

'You'll learn,' she said softly. 'You'll learn a lot of things, Kip. And when it comes time, you'll help me pay him back, the way it will hurt him most.'

## CHAPTER TEN

Kip's piebald drifted back to its home ranch two days later. It was still saddled. A Three Dot puncher found it and brought it in, and Verne Mathis checked it.

There was no blood on the saddle, nor had the animal been hurt. The gun and cartridge belt he had given Kip were still in the saddle bag. He shook his head, his eyes hard.

'He might have just turned him loose, Mr. Westwood,' he said. 'But I have a hunch he didn't—'

Brent Westwood put his gaze on the distant hills. He wondered what had happened to the jaunty boy who had left Three Dot—a strange youngster with a cap pulled low over his eyes.

'Better let Deputy Tom Gallen know, Verne,' he suggested.

Verne rode into town that afternoon. He

found Tom Gallen in his office, reading a letter. The deputy looked up as Verne crossed the threshold, and he crumpled the letter and dropped it into his wastebasket. His eyes met Verne's.

'Rocking V been annoyin' you, Verne?'

'Not yet,' Verne said. 'And we'll handle it when they do.' He sat on the edge of Tom's desk and pushed his hat back on his forehead. His roan mustache drooped a little at the corners of his grooved mouth.

'The kid's run into trouble,' he said. 'You seen Vic or Chinook around lately?'

Tom Gallen's eyes narrowed. 'Why?'

Verge told him about the piebald. 'He got back at them both before he left. They don't look like the breed of rattlesnake to forget, Tom.'

Tom Gallen settled back, a sigh escaping him. 'I told him to leave the country,' he muttered. He looked up at the Three Dot foreman. 'What do you expect me to do?'

'It's yore job,' Verne pointed out bluntly. 'The kid was headed for Yellow Horse. That's still in yore territory, Tom. Somethin' happened to him——'

'The piebald might've thrown him!' Tom muttered harshly. 'You consider that?'

Verne nodded. 'But I'm bettin' that he didn't. Thought I'd tell you about it. If you don't do anythin' about it, Mr. Westwood said to find the kid. We'll ride Three Dot to Yellow

122

Horse. If he ain't there, we'll ride to Rockin'
V—'

'You'll ride nowhere!' Gallen snapped. He
came out of his chair and reached for his hat.
His left arm was still in a sling, but he was too
restless to take things easy. 'I'll take a ride up
to Yellow Horse. The kid's probably up there
with his brother.'

'Tell him we got the piebald back then,'
Verne said, and turned away. He walked out of
the office and stood in the middle of the quiet
street and watched Malvina Havison turn her
buggy in to Abe Mosher's Mercantile Store
rack. He eyed her with detached curiosity. He
seldom saw any of the Havison girls; since
Brian's disappearance he had not seen Meg
Havison in town at all.

He recalled riding out to the Havison place
with Mr. Westwood and Tom Gallen, the day
after the disappearance of Brian. Meg had
been sick then, he remembered. Some kind of
shock, Doc Spooner had said.

He watched Malvina dismount and stride
into the store. She was dressed like a man and
looked like a man, from a distance. The Smith
and Wesson she wore at her right hip helped
the illusion.

He turned and mounted his cayuse and rode
over to the bank where workmen were
rebuilding the bank front. Crawford was
standing outside, watching them. The banker
was a man of medium height, with dark brown

hair and light blue eyes. A worried man.

He saw Verne and nodded a greeting, and the Three Dot ramrod pulled up and slid out of the saddle. He watched the workmen in silence for a moment.

Crawford said: 'One more raid like that and I'm ruined.' His voice was sour. 'I wired the sheriff. Haven't even gotten the courtesy of an answer.'

Verne glanced at the poster newly tacked to the side of the building. 'Heard they upped the reward for Kansas to five thousand dollars. That it?'

Crawford nodded, 'Banker's Association is putting up the money. Might attract some bounty hunters, anyway.' His voice was bitter. 'We pay the law for protection against this sort of thing; then we have to put up more money to get the job done.'

Verne shrugged. 'How much did Kansas get?'

'Thirty-two thousand dollars, near as I can get it figured out.' Crawford shook his head. 'I've got the money covered. But—' He looked at the Three Dot foreman, his brow furrowing with concern. 'What's this trouble between you and Monte Cozzens?'

'Range trouble,' Verne answered briefly. 'Monte Cozzens has decided he hasn't got enough of Antelope Valley. He's spreadin' out—at Three Dot's expense.' Verne's voice held a bleak anger. 'Mr. Westwood's a gentleman, and a patient man. I'm not.'

Crawford sighed. 'Darn fools, both of you. As if Kansas isn't giving us enough trouble. What will Monte get out of a range war—?'

'He'll get a piece of land,' Verne said sourly, 'six foot long and three feet deep.' He turned and mounted his horse and nodded briefly. 'Good day, Mr. Crawford.'

He rode slowly out of town, his anger still running deep. Brent Westwood's money was in England and not affected by Kansas' raid on the bank. He knew this, and knew that it would not be financial trouble which would push Westwood. He considered the phony Judge Weller and wondered who the Judge was fronting for. Monte Cozzens? Monte was the logical man to want Three Dot. It made sense that way. Start trouble; then try to buy Three Dot from behind the camouflage of a man like Judge Weller.

But somehow he couldn't make it ring true. And because it didn't, uncertainty nagged at him. There was more behind the threat of a range war with Rocking V than appeared on the surface. Somehow Kansas and Rocking V and the attempt on Brent Westwood's life fitted together—it was like a jigsaw puzzle with a couple of pieces missing. Even Brian Westwood's strange disappearance was part of the pattern. He fitted in somewhere . . .

He glanced up as a rider jogged into sight around a bend in the trail. The smoldering

125

anger in him broke into a sneer of anticipation. He reined in and waited for Vic Canny, who sat straight in the saddle, his shoulders stiff, his eyes wary.

'Ridin' into town again?' Verne greeted him grimly. 'My, my—Monte is sure soft with his riders. Pays a full month's wages for ten days' work. Or is he paying you for special jobs only? Like ambushin', for instance?'

'I've got business in town!' Vic snarled. His eyes had a trapped, scared look. He knew Verne Mathis' reputation with a gun, and he wasn't about to be drawn into a shootout here. The Three Dot ramrod saw the fear in Vic's eyes, and contempt was in his voice.

'Sorta lost without that gunslingin' partner of yores, ain't you?' he baited grimly. 'Chinook do yore thinkin' for you, too?'

'I do my own thinkin' an' my own talkin'!' Vic snapped. His voice was thin, desperate. He tried to edge his mount around the man in the road, but Verne cut him off.

'You probably got Tom Gallen fooled,' Verne said harshly, 'but you didn't fool me. Kip Nunninger saw you an' Chinook at that water tower an' you know it. I'm callin' you a liar an' a yellow-bellied coward to boot! An' if you've got any guts you'll go for that iron you pack on yore hip!'

Vic's face went white. His lips trembled. 'I don't want trouble with you,' he said doggedly. 'I wasn't there at the water tower. The kid was—'

'Yo're a liar!' Verne snapped.

Vic stiffened. Hate traced its ugly pattern in his thin face. But he put his head down and clasped his hands at the back of his neck. 'I ain't drawin' on you,' he whispered. His tone was abject, whimpering. 'I got business in town. I ain't drawin' on you.'

Verne leaned over and slapped his face. The blow rocked the redheaded gunster back. It left its white imprint on the tan of his cheek.

The Rocking V gunman's eyes met Verne's with dark, bitter hatred. 'I'll pay you for that, Verne! But not now—not here!' He kneed his mount past the Three Dot ramrod then, and Verne let him by, a sneer on his face.

\*       \*       \*

Deputy Sheriff Tom Gallen saw Malvina Havison come out of Abe's store and climb into her buggy and drive off. She smiled and nodded briefly, and he touched his hat, wondering what had brought her to town. They were a clannish group, the Havison sisters. Something not right about them. He had a bachelor's distrust of women, especially spinsters. The oldest one, Nora, was a bit touched, people said. She kept to herself, was seldom seen. Even in the days when Gunn Havison, cognizant of his duty to his daughters, had invited eligible men to dinner,

127

Nora Havison had kept to herself.

Meg Havison was different. Right pretty girl, that Meg, for a Havison. Funny about her. Or maybe not so funny, he thought. She and young Brian Westwood had seemed right close, although Brian had been seeing a lot of Sally Mason, too. Still, it was understandable that Meg had a shock right after Brian had disappeared.

But Malvina—there was a hard one. She walked like a man and talked like one, and could shoot like a man, too. He watched the buggy disappear toward the low hills to the north, and then he turned and headed for the stables.

Abe Mosher had come to the doorway. He was a short, fat man and he perspired a lot. He was wearing a black band on his arm, in mourning for his son. He mopped his face with a handkerchief, and when Gallen paused, he commented shrewdly: 'Now what would Malvina Havison be buying shirts and pants for?'

Gallen had his own troubles; his answer was mechanical. 'She wears pants. Wears 'em right well, too.' Then he frowned and looked up as Abe said sharply: 'She bought ten boxes of ammunition, too. .45 caliber.'

'Ammunition, eh?' Tom shook his head. 'Might be she's expectin' trouble.'

'She wears a .38,' Abe pointed out, a fact Deputy Sheriff Gallen was aware of.

'Might be she wants to melt them down,' Gallen muttered, and walked off. He didn't want to gossip with Abe about the Havison girl; he had other things troubling him.

Abe watched him stride off and scratched his bald head. 'Melt them down, eh?' he muttered. 'Tom must be losing his mind.' Then he heard his wife call and turned back inside the store.

At the Straw Stables, Tom Gallen had Jed Peters saddle his buckskin for him. John Straw watched from his seat on the bench.

'Goin' ridin'?'

'Need the air,' Gallen said shortly. He was getting close-mouthed, he realized, but his bitterness was like a sour thing in him, eating at him like an ulcer.

'Two canteens of water,' he told Jed, and heard Straw snort.

'Need the air, eh? Two canteens of water. A man kin breathe all the air 'tween here an' the Sleepers on two canteens of water.' He eyed Tom shrewdly. 'You goin' after Kansas alone?'

'I'm mindin' my own business!' Gallen snapped.

John Straw's teeth ground hard on his pipestem. He looked at Tom mount and he said angrily: 'Hope yore business chokes yuh—' and watched Tom ride off.

Tom Gallen knew the way and he had a good horse, and he made Yellow Horse just after dark. He came up the narrow winding road feeling the gulch walls hem him in, blot out the stars. He rode slack in the saddle, a hard, taciturn man who had known this town when it was lusty and brawling and when Christy Conway had been its day marshal and Bill Stevens had nailed down the night watch. It was the time when Santa Fe ran two trains daily to this depot; when men in rough miner's clothes talked of millions and their women, taking in washing one day, hiring servants the next. It was a town with memories gone sour— it was a dangerous town because it should have died a year ago.

But he had to know what he had come for. Kip Nunninger had ridden up here to find his brother, and his horse had returned, saddled but riderless, to Three Dot. Maybe there was nothing to it. But it was his job to make sure.

He rode up the dark weed-grown street, past a tar-papered shack where a man, about to push through the slatted doors, went still and quiet, staring at Tom Gallen as though he were seeing things. Then he ducked inside, and Tom Gallen was suddenly aware of the metal symbol on his vest and felt a prickle run down his back.

He rode up the dark and silent street and pulled up at the sagging rail of the Yellow Horse Hotel and went inside.

Abigail came out of an inner room as he walked to the desk. She was an unhandsome woman and she eyed his star with distrust. He

130

saw no surprise in her eyes, and he knew his coming must have been telegraphed to every shady citizen inhabiting this relic of a gold camp.

'Collectin' taxes again?' she muttered.

'You know it ain't time,' he said. 'I'm lookin' for a man—not more than a boy, I reckon. Name's Kip Nunninger.'

She started to shake her head, saw him reach for the register and shrugged. 'He was here. He left the followin' mornin'.'

Tom frowned. 'Did he meet up with his brother?'

'Who?'

'Brother. He came to Yellow Horse to find his brother. Fred Nunninger.'

'Oh!' Abigail glanced toward the staircase. Her husband, Jake, appeared, dragging his foot. He came toward them, eyeing Tom's star.

The woman's voice grew harsh. 'The boy's brother left town more than a year ago. He didn't leave word where he was goin'. I told the boy that. He was plumb disappointed. He left the next mornin'—'

'Then he didn't see his brother?'

'I told ye,' the woman snapped. She brushed a strand of iron gray hair back from her face. 'I'm cleanin' up in the kitchen. I ain't got time to gab with you.'

Jake said: 'Might invite the deppity in for somethin' to eat, seein' as how he had a long ride for nothin'.'

'I could stand a bite,' Tom nodded. 'An' I'll want a room, too—just for the night.'

He had the strong feeling that this woman knew what had happened to Kip Nunninger, but he knew, too, she would not talk. He went up to his room and washed and came back down to the kitchen where Abigail set out a plate of left-over beefsteaks and potatoes. He ate slowly, surprised to find he was hungry.

Jake, who was helping with the dishes, said: 'Nice feller, that boy. Rode a fine animal, too. Piebald, branded Three Dot W.' Jake turned and eyed Tom questioningly. 'He work for Three Dot? Or was he a hoss thief?'

'Neither one,' Tom said. He settled back and made himself a smoke. He could use the fingers of his left hand, but they were stiff, and moving them hurt.

The woman turned an impatient eye toward him. 'You lookin' for him because of that arm? He cause you trouble?'

Tom shook his head. 'Jest a sprain,' he lied. 'Kid was a friend of mine.' He looked at Jake. 'When did the kid leave?'

Jake made a gesture with his hands. 'Heck, I don't know. He went up to his room 'bout ten thirty, I guess. He wasn't there when I got up. I get up early, too, with the sun. I went into the barn an' saw his hoss was gone, so I went up an' looked in his room. He was gone.'

'Then he left here ridin' the piebald?'

'Wal,' Jake scowled, 'can't rightly say he did.

I say he was gone an' the piebald was gone. Might be they left together. Seems logical.'

Gallen nodded. 'Reckon it does.'

He rose and walked out of the kitchen, through the dingy lobby, and paused on the veranda to watch the stars burning in the narrow velvet strip of sky overhead. Music from the Red Devil Saloon which he had passed on the way there drifted to him, and curiosity rode him. He walked down the plank walk, avoided the broken boards, and pushed his way through the slatted doors.

There was a smoke haze in the low-ceilinged room and the sour smell of spilled beer. A few miners sat around a poker table. Several rag-tag gunmen were ranged along the bar, clapping time to the music of a guitar player. A Mexican girl was tapping out a fast dance rhythm.

The guitar player, an out-at-the-elbows Mexican, ran his thumb across the strings in a harsh finale and turned to scowl at him. The girl stopped dancing, her eyes quickening with fear and excitement.

Gallen said: 'Keep on with the fun.' He touched his badge. 'I'll take it off if it bothers yuh, gal.'

The guitar player glanced toward the men at the bar. One of them, a slim, dark Mexican, nodded silently. The guitarist plucked at his strings. The girl tossed her head in defiance and began to dance.

But the atmosphere in the Red Devil was suddenly subdued; it lacked the rough geniality it had before the lawman's coming. Gallen had a beer at the bar. He would have been willing to risk a month's pay betting that some of these hardcases were members of Kansas' outlaw bunch. But he had no proof. And he had not come here to play a lone hand. He drank his beer and paid for it and was about to leave when Judge Weller walked in. The judge had been drinking somewhere else, for he staggered slightly as he came through the doors, and his eyes had a glazed look. He came up to the rail beside Gallen without noticing the lawman and put both hands flat on the counter.

Gallen turned and put his cold, questioning gaze on this man who was supposed to be at the county seat.

'Evenin', Judge,' he said bleakly.

Judge Weller shrank back, shock paling his florid features. He gulped visibly. 'Evening, Gallen,' he mumbled. Then he recovered his composure and straightened up, his chest thrusting out like a pouter pigeon. 'Evening,' he repeated loudly. He banged his fist on the bar. 'Your best bourbon, sir. For my good friend, Deputy Sheriff Tom Gallen. Your very best bourbon, bartender.'

The man behind the bar scowled. He took the bottle he had been using for the others and banged it in front of the Judge and placed a glass in front of him. 'That's the best likker you'll get here—an' it ain't bourbon!'

'Ah, me!' the Judge sighed. '"Let us not burden our remembrances with a heaviness that's gone . . ."' He turned to Gallen. 'Shakespeare, sir. Did I ever tell you I toured Europe with the Spencer Players?'

Tom shook his head. 'Thought you were a judge,' he said acridly.

The pompous man caught himself. 'In later years, sir—in later years.' He drank the fiery whiskey in front of him and asked for a refill. His eyes held a narrow shrewdness as he appraised Gallen.

'Quite a surprise to see you here, sir.'

'Quite,' Tom agreed dryly. 'I thought you had gone to Meridian.'

Judge Weller licked hislips. 'Last minute change in plans, sir. A business matter.'

'Business? Here?' Tom looked around him. He saw that the slim Mexican with the two tied-down guns was frowning, and he felt tension growing in the room.

'Well, yes, business,' Weller said. 'A matter of a mining claim. I represent a client who's interested in the old Barr mine.'

'You have many clients, Judge?' Tom murmured. 'Or is this client you represent the same man who's been wanting to buy out Three Dot?'

Judge Weller drew himself up. 'Such a supposition is unfounded and misleading, sir. I am a man of integrity and honor—'

'I said nothin' about honor,' Tom broke in. 'But tell me, just what are you doin' here?'

Weller stuck out his lower lip in a gesture of defiance. 'Business.' He took a step back from the bar and tucked his right hand beneath his coat, Napoleon-style. ' "There is a tide in the affairs of men, sir, which, taken at the flood, leads on to fortune—" '

'There's a tide that leaves a lot of stinkin' seaweed behind, too,' Gallen said bluntly. He ignored the drink at his elbow. 'Evenin', Judge. I shall see you again, in my office, about this business you have here.'

Weller nodded. 'By all means, sir,' he said, and watched the lawman step away from the bar. The door swung shut behind Gallen, and the silence was suddenly harsh with the discords of the guitar.

Keno walked up to the judge, who was pouring himself another drink. He knocked the drink out of the man's hand, and Weller turned and shrank away from the killer.

'I didn't know he'd be here,' he whined. 'Nobody told me—'

Keno said: 'Get out! Get back to Kansas. Tell him what happened. Tell him—' his eyes glittered—'that I'll take care of the lawman!'

\*     \*     \*

Tom Gallen left Yellow Horse early the next

136

morning. He rode out of town as the pink flush of sunrise painted the top of the gulch wall.

He rode with a sense of foreboding he couldn't shake off. Not even the brightness of the day, the cool and invigorating chill of morning, lifted his spirits.

He had not found Kip, and now he was sure something had happened to the kid. But why? If the kid had not found his brother, what had he run into? Why would anyone want to kill him, a complete stranger?

Tom Gallen had a strong hunch that Kansas and his men hung out in Yellow Horse. He couldn't prove it. And it didn't mean much, his knowing. Alone, he would have been killed the moment he stepped out of line and began making noises like a lawman. And he knew that a posse would be spotted long before it reached Yellow Horse, and that the posse, when it arrived, would find Yellow Horse without a trace of the gunmen he had seen in the Red Devil Saloon last night.

This was something he couldn't handle alone. He knew this, and then he thought of the youngster he had come to find and he shook his head. 'Sorry, Kip,' he muttered. 'You should never have come up here in the first place.'

He came out of the Sleepers with the sun two hours high. He came to the point where the overgrown trail met and ran alongside the rusted iron rails of the Santa Fe spur. He stopped here to let the buckskin rest. The sun felt good on his back and he reached in his pocket for the makings.

The rifle bullet smashed into his spine, just below the back of his neck!

He fell forward, dead before he touched the pommel. The buckskin shied at the sharp whipcrack of the rifle, and Tom tilted sideways and slumped out of the saddle. The animal broke into a frightened run and then, as it found the morning still, its fright died quickly and it stopped and began cropping at spiky grass.

After a few bites it drifted back to the huddled figure on the trail and stood over him, waiting.

Up on the rock ledge overlooking the road and the iron rails, Keno eased back. He had waited a long time for Tom Gallen to show up, and he felt stiff. He worked his fingers, and a smile slid across his dark face.

His job was half done.

He went down and caught the buckskin and piled the deputy's body across the saddle. Then he led the burdened animal away, trailing it behind him as he headed away from the road toward the naked, inhospitable hills.

There were places in the Sleepers, Keno knew, where a man and a horse could be dropped and not be found in a hundred years . . .

# CHAPTER ELEVEN

Kip Nunninger learned quickly. He had natural coordination, speed and a grim motivation for learning. And he had a good teacher.

It seemed odd, at first, that Malvina Havison should be the one to show him how to handle the big Peacemaker that had belonged to her father. Yet the woman knew her guns.

'We'll start with stationary targets first,' she said. 'Draw and shoot . . . draw . . . draw . . . Aiming isn't important in a close fight. And most gun arguments are at close quarters. You'll have to get that gun out and cocked before the other fellow . . . get it out and fire. You save time by cocking the hammer with your thumb as you draw. You let the hammer fall as you bring up the muzzle . . . like this, Kip . . . like this . . .'

She drew and fired the .38 and fired again, and Kip nodded slowly. It came fast, as though he had always had it in him, this gun speed.

He had changed externally, too. He wore Gunner Havison's gray Stetson and the blue cotton shirt and Levis that Malvina had bought in town. Malvina bought him boots on her second trip to town for more ammunition.

He did his chores and practiced afterward. Malvina worked with him, as though she had a definite purpose in helping him. Her satisfaction seemed to increase with his progress.

Nora Havison stayed out of the way. Once she had come around the barn and caught Kip just as he banged away at a tomato can. She clapped her hands to her ears and ran back to the house, her face white. He didn't see her for almost two days afterward.

Meg didn't interfere. Kip saw her sitting and rocking in the house, but she didn't react to him at all. Both sisters catered to her, treated her like a child. Yet she wasn't physically ill. She looked healthy. She ate well. But her eyes had a strange dull luster and there was no ambition in her. She rocked and looked out of the window. Sometimes she read . . .

Kip did his chores. He rode the hills and brought back Broken Quirt strays, some of which had never seen a branding iron. He learned to put a hot iron on the flank of a roped maverick. Malvina worked with him, showing him, telling him. He learned a lot in two weeks.

On the fifteenth day he stood on the veranda, looking toward the blue shadow of the Sleepers. He had cut himself off from the world around; he had lived within the narrow purposes of life here on Broken Quirt.

It was time to go.

Malvina joined him. He had told her the night before he would be leaving. She had not tried to get him to stay, but some of the brightness went out of her. Now she looked tired, as though she had slept badly. Her voice was without inflection as she asked: 'You still want to get Kansas, don't you?'

He nodded grimly, and his hand slid down over the now familiar bone handle of the Peacemaker. 'He killed my brother, Miss Havison. Bragged about it to my face—'

She looked away, an odd light in her eyes. 'Maybe he was lying, Kip.'

'Why? Why should he lie about it?'

She shrugged. 'Perhaps he'll tell you, when you see him again.' She walked with him to the corral, where he saddled Vanity. 'I'll leave her down at the Straw Stables, as you wish,' he said. 'Thanks for everything, Miss Havison.'

She held out her hand and shook his, like a man.

The road curved out of sight of the yard under the creek bluffs and Kip pulled aside, neck-reining Vanity, as Nora Havison came down the steep path leading to the Havison cemetery. She saw him and stood shyly, her eyes downcast.

He rode to her and took off his hat and said: 'Goodbye, Nora. I've never enjoyed cooking as much as yours. Look—' He thumbed his middle and grinned. 'I'm getting fat.'

She giggled. It was a strange sound coming from her. Then she looked up and he saw tears in her eyes.

'Goodbye, Kip. It's been nice to have a man around to cook for.' She turned away, like some schoolgirl caught with her first beau. She took a few quick steps, then turned to face him, and now her face had changed again. There was a sharp concern in her eyes.

'Please don't tell anyone, Kip. About him up there.'

'Who?'

'Brian. He—Meg didn't mean to kill him—' She lifted a hand to her mouth, and her eyes were wide and dark with sudden terror. 'Oh . . . oh . . .' And then she turned and ran down the road to the yard.

*　　　*　　　*

Memory of Nora Havison's broken, frightened face remained with Kip Nunninger as he headed toward town. Brian? The strange, unmarked grave on the hill, in a corner, away from the other Havisons. The grave with the fresh flowers.

Brian Westwood?

He shook his head. It could be. And it occurred to Kip that it would explain Meg's strange behavior. And it explained Malvina's and Nora's careful handling of her.

He felt cold, although the sun was warm on his face. He felt like a man who had suddenly poked into a crypt and found himself staring at old bones. He felt sorry for the Havison

142

women. Nora, homely and shy, a wonderful cook, a kindly person living a quiet death on a broken-down ranch. Malvina, too strong-willed, too hard for a woman . . . with some strange secret of her own.

Kip felt torn between his gratitude to them and what he now knew. Or was he sure? Malvina Havison would deny everything, and Nora would retreat into stony silence. And what would exposing their secret do to Meg?

If it was really Brian Westwood up on that hill, let him lie.

But Brent Westwood ought to know. It would end the man's eternal vigil, his waiting. Painful as it would be, the knowledge would finally set him free.

Kip Nunninger rode into town with this weighing on him.

John Straw was shoveling manure into a pile when Kip rode Vanity up the ramp into the barn. The old man's jaw dropped. The pipe he had been holding between his teeth fell into the manure at his feet. He picked it up, brushed it off mechanically, and thrust it between his teeth again.

Kip greeted him cheerfully. 'Howdy, Pop. Working for a change?'

John Straw leaned on his pitchfork. 'You back?' His voice was thin, cracked and defensive. 'Where's Tom Gallen?'

Kip's grin faded. 'The deputy with the sour face? How would I know?'

143

John Straw leaned the pitchfork against the wall and mopped his face with a dirty handkerchief. 'Country's shore goin' to the dogs,' he mumbled.

Kip slid out of the saddle. He walked up to Straw, leading Vanity. 'Where is Deputy Gallen?'

'Out lookin' for you!' the old man snapped. His eyes glinted at the humor of the situation. 'Verne Mathis an' a passel of Three Dot riders are out lookin' fer Tom.' He cocked his head like an old, bedraggled rooster and blinked his eyes. 'Reg'lar peerade out there. Everybody's gone to Yeller Horse.' He started to chuckle, then ran his gaze over Kip, his eyes narrowing suspiciously.

'What's happened to you, son? Didn't strike me right off, seein' you in thet big hat an' range getup. Keeripes, you gone loco?'

'Got wise, maybe,' Kip answered. He handed the old man Vanity's reins. 'Miss Havison said to leave her with you until she comes to town. I'll be needing a cayuse of my own. You have an animal I can hire? Or buy?'

Straw scratched his head. 'Danged if I kin understand all this, son. First time I laid eyes on yuh, you was ridin' a Three Dot piebald. Now yuh show up on a Broken Quirt animal—Malvina Havison's own special cayuse, too.' He wagged his head suspiciously. 'Yuh shore you don't know what happened to Tom Gallen?'

144

'Haven't seen Gallen since the morning I left town,' Kip replied. He paused in the doorway. 'What made Tom ride out to Yellow Horse after me?'

Straw sniffed. 'Three Dot ramrod rode into town. Said thet piebald you been ridin' showed up at the ranch without yuh, still saddled. Was 'bout three days after you left town.' Straw took his pipe from his mouth and spat into the manure pile. 'You shore caused a rumpus, son. Tom's been gone more than a week now. Verne Mathis an' his boys headed for the Sleepers couple of days ago . . .'

Kip frowned. 'Hope they enjoy the ride,' he said coldly. He didn't like all the fuss that seemed to have been stirred up because he had gone to Yellow Horse. What had happened to him was his own private business; it was between him and Kansas.

He went outside, stepping into the late morning sun, and the glare made him squint. People turned to look at him as he walked by. As he paused on the corner to cross the street to the Bonnie Bonnet, a man with a badge on his greasy vest stepped out to intercept him. The lawman had a wooden peg for his left leg, and a Colt strapped to his right hip, and he wore a Confederate military cap over a balding gray head.

'Jest a minnit, son!'

Kip turned. The lawman looked him over coldly, and Kip recognized him as the man

145

who had brought his piebald around to the front of the lunchroom the morning he had had coffee with Tom Gallen.

'You the kid Tom called Kip Nunninger?'

Kip nodded.

Jed Peters looked him over. Wearing the badge had given him a dignity he had not had before. He stood straighter and his eyes were steadier.

'I'm holdin' down the law here,' he said, 'until Tom gets back. He rode out to Yeller Horse lookin' for you—'

'So I heard,' Kip cut him off coldly.

'Wal . . . ?'

'I'm sorry I caused the law trouble!' Kip snapped. He was irritated at the turn of events. He saw Jed's gray eyes chill.

'Mebbe you got a heap of explainin' to do, son,' the lawman growled.

'I don't think so,' Kip answered harshly. He started to turn away, and Jed dropped his hand to his Colt. Kip whirled. The Peacemaker came up fast, its muzzle an inch from Jed's belt buckle. The man gasped and backed away, his face whitening. He pulled his hand away from his Colt and dropped it by his side.

'I've got other things on my mind,' Kip snapped. 'I haven't got time to explain to every old fool where I've gone and why I'm back. This is a free country. I didn't ask Tom Gallen to ride to Yellow Horse after me. If he wanted to stick his nose into my business, that's his problem. Don't you follow his bad example.'

Jed was stiff. 'Reckon it is yore business,' he admitted. 'But if somethin's happened to Tom, I'll be askin' you questions again!'

Kip shrugged. He left the lawman and crossed the street. The thought of seeing Sally Mason again warmed him. After the Havison women Sally's frank femininity would be welcome.

He paused on the walk by the curtained lunchroom window, and thought how familiar this was, and how far away San Francisco seemed. The distant hills still held their mysterious aloofness, but they were no longer alien. The wide sweep of Antelope Valley was familiar now, as were its problems . . . He was smiling as he opened the door and stepped inside.

The bell jangled. Sally Mason was arranging cheesecloth over a row of freshly baked pies on the back shelf. She finished her job and turned to see who had come in. Kip was settling on a stool when she faced him.

He saw shock on her face, and then came gladness, lighting up her eyes. 'Kip—Kip—you're back—' She turned crimson then with the knowledge that there was more in her voice and in her eyes than she had intended to show him.

He said lightly: 'I didn't realize I would be missed or I would have dropped in earlier, Sally.'

147

She forced her features into normal composure. 'You know that Tom Gallen is out looking for you?' she said. There was accusation in her tone now, to cover up her confusion.

'I heard,' he said carelessly.

'What happened to you?'

'Pour me a cup of coffee, please,' he said, smiling. 'I'll tell you all about it.'

She pursed her lips at him. 'Bossy, aren't you? And I see you're wearing a big hat—' She leaned over the counter, the teasing light fading from her face. 'A gun, too, Kip?' There was alarm in her voice now. 'What's happened to you?'

'The coffee first,' he repeated firmly.

She tossed her head and turned. She poured coffee into a mug from the pot, and Kip watched the back of her neck, liking the way she held herself. When she turned he noticed the look in her eyes. They were troubled and concerned, and her lower lip trembled slightly as she placed the mug on the counter in front of him.

In that moment frivolity left him; he wanted to get up and take hold of her and reassure her.

'Did you find your brother?'

He settled back on the stool and shook his head. 'I didn't find him, Sally. But I found the man who killed him!'

Just outside of town, Verne Mathis and his men halted at the fork in the road. Behind them were the long miles to Yellow Horse, the fruitless miles.

Verne put his glance on the somber-faced Powell riding at his side. 'I'm goin' into town, Red,' he said tiredly. 'You an' the boys ride back to the ranch. Tell Mister Westwood we found nothin'. Tell him that the kid an' Tom Gallen ain't never goin' to come back. They're dead. We can't prove it. But tell him, Red . . .'

He reined aside and watched them ride. He had done what Brent Westwood had 'wanted, although he had argued against leaving the ranch with half its crew during this period of crisis with Rocking V. He didn't trust Monte Cozzens, and he had a hunch that the trouble between them was coming to a head. He couldn't place his finger on anything, but he didn't like what had happened these past weeks.

The kid didn't figure in it, as far as he could see. Just a youngster who had happened to be in the way at the wrong time. But Brent had a sense of honor and obligation; he felt he owed Kip Nunninger his life. And he had insisted that Verne try to find out what had happened to him.

But Tom Gallen's disappearance bothered

149

Verne. In a way the Three Dot ramrod felt responsible for the deputy. It was he who had egged Tom Gallen into riding to Yellow Horse.

He had found no trace of Gallen, either on the road to the mining camp or at the gulch town. Abigail admitted readily enough that Tom Gallen had been there—had even spent the night. But she insisted Tom had ridden back the following morning, and she stuck to her story.

It was the same story she told about Kip. The kid had showed up and asked about his brother. She had remembered that a Fred Nunninger had stayed at the hotel, but he had left over a year ago. Fred had left no address where he could be reached. She had told Kip that, and he had left Yellow Horse early the next morning. No, neither she nor Jake, her husband, had seen the kid leave. But his horse was gone from the stall where Jake had put him, so they had assumed he had saddled and ridden off.

That was all Verne had gotten out of the long ride to Yellow Horse. A dead camp, rotting between the gulch walls that hemmed it in.

He couldn't prove that Tom Gallen was dead, but deep inside, Verne knew. And he felt that the sheriff at Meridian should be told what had happened. Jed Peters, part time deputy, had taken over in Tom's absence. It would be Jed's job to wire the sheriff.

Verne scowled at this. Rocking V couldn't have a better opportunity, if it wanted to make trouble now. Jed was no lawman. With Tom Gallen gone, the law was seventy long miles away. It could be on the other side of the moon; he thought grimly, as far as its effectiveness in Antelope Valley went.

He was thinking this as he rode down No Water Street, and he didn't see John Straw wave to him. Nor did he pay attention to the two Rocking V cayuses tied up at the rack before the Three Deuces Saloon, or glimpse Vic Canny watching him over the slatted doors. He reined in before the law office, a tired, dusty man, and tied up. He stamped into the office and paused to slap dust from his clothes.

Jed Peters was behind Tom's desk, scowling at the new dodger on Kansas. There was no picture of the outlaw; just a vague description. A short, stocky man, somewhere between twenty and forty years old. Brown hair, gray-green eyes. Wore two Colts, walnut handles, .45 caliber. Wore a blue bandanna over his face. $5,000 reward was offered for information leading to his capture and conviction . . .

Jed looked up as Verne leaned over the desk.

'No sign of Tom,' the Three Dot ramrod said bluntly. 'Yellow Horse was dead as last year's blow flies. A handful of miners, that's

151

all. We talked with the woman who runs the fleabag hotel. She said Tom was there. Stayed the night and rode away—'

Jed picked at his teeth with his thumb nail. 'You see the kid?'

'No. The woman told the same story about him. Got there, asked about his brother. When he was told his brother had left Yellow Horse a year ago, he pulled out—'

'I mean now,' Jed interrupted coldly. 'The kid's in town. Ran into him not more'n fifteen minutes ago.' His lips curled. 'Didn't recognize him right off. He's changed them clothes he wore. Reg'lar range hand now. An' this'll mebbe surprise yuh, Verne. He's packin' a gun, a Peacemaker Colt.' His voice raised sharply at the doubting look in Verne's eyes. 'An' so help me, Mathis, he's good with it!'

Verne straightened and backed off from the desk. He rubbed his stubbled jaw with the back of his hand. 'You been drinkin' again, Jed?'

'Not while I wear this star!' Jed said angrily. 'I saw the kid! He's in the Bonnie Bonnet now!'

Verne frowned. 'Mebbe we oughta have a talk with him, Jed.'

Jed licked his lips and settled back in his chair. 'I'm warnin' yuh, Mathis—the kid's dangerous. He told me he ain't talkin—'

'He'll talk to me!' Verne cut in harshly. His hand brushed down over his gun. 'He'll talk to me, Jed, so help me!'

He walked out, his anger short-lived. He didn't expect trouble with the kid. He paused on the walk in front of the law office.

Vic Canny stepped out of the alley less than twenty feet away.

'Verne!' he said sharply.

The Three Dot foreman made no sudden move. He saw the Rocking V gunslinger out of the corner of his eye, and he knew that Vic was set to kill. Then his attention was caught by the tall, stoop-shouldered man who moved into the middle of the street from the doorway across the road.

Chinook!

They had him between them. Whipsawed!

Vic Canny eased up onto the boardwalk, made bold by the presence of his partner. He faced Verne, a lean, dangerous man now that he had the odds with him.

Jed had clumped to the door. He saw Verne standing rigid at the edge of the plank walk, and it took a few moments before he realized the situation.

Chinook's cold ugly voice cracked down hard. 'Jed! Get back inside! Stay clear of this!'

Jed hesitated. His face slowly turned the color of old coffee. He looked at Verne with apology in his eyes. Then he backed inside.

Vic's voice flung its thin challenge to the Three Dot ramrod. 'I'm callin' the turn now, Mathis! I'm callin' you a liar an' a yeller-livered—'

153

Verne drew. He had his Colt out when Chinook's lead hit him in the side. It spoiled his first shot. Vic's lead brushed him as he went down to one knee. He kept his muzzle up and thumbed the hammer twice. He saw Vic reach up on his toes, and his scream of pain was high and thin in the afternoon.

Then Chinook's lead killed him.

## CHAPTER TWELVE

Kip was finishing telling his story to Sally when the lunchroom door opened and a man backed in. The newcomer turned and looked at them, his face tense.

'Gunfight out there,' he said excitedly. 'Rocking V punchers got Verne Mathis boxed between them!'

Kip swung off his stool. He was halfway to the door when the first shot broke the afternoon quiet. He shoved aside the man who was peering through the glass panel in the door and stepped out onto the walk in time to see Verne Mathis die.

Chinook was crouched in the middle of the street some fifteen feet from Kip. Vic Canny had fallen against the wooden canopy post and was clinging to it, like some drunk . . .

Kip's voice reached out to the Rocking V gunman with an icy challenge. 'Chinook!

Count me in!'

The horse-faced killer whirled. He saw Kip on the walk in front of the lunchroom and recognized him in spite of the change in clothes. He flipped the smoking muzzle of his right Colt up and was careless with his first and only shot.

He didn't see Kip draw. He felt a hammer blow against his chest, and he staggered and tried to lift his gun again. Kip's second bullet spilled him into the dust of the street. Kip glanced back at the broken window where Chinook's lead had gone; then he stepped off into the street and ran to Verne Mathis. The Three Dot ramrod was lying on his side, his knees pulled up toward his chest. Kip turned him over and saw that Verne was already dead.

Vic Canny had slid down along the post. He lay against it, his eyes open but dulled and unseeing. His breathing was jerky.

Men began walking toward the scene. Doctor Spooner, hatless and coatless, came hurrying down the walk. He crossed over to Chinook and didn't even stop. He passed the man with only a quick downward glance and came to where Kip was standing over Verne. He bent over the Three Dot ramrod, then straightened and shook his head. He walked to Vic, pulled the man's shirt open, away from the sticky mess of blood, and muttered: 'This one might live awhile—'

Kip didn't move. The shock of what had

155

happened was beginning to penetrate through to him. He looked down at Verne Mathis, and it was no longer the hard, capable Three Dot ramrod he saw, but a body in old dusty clothes. He felt a little sick. He turned away, his face white, and walked blindly back across the street . . .

Jed Peters came out of the office. He stood by Verne's body, an ineffectual man made helpless and ashamed by the cowardice he had just shown. He felt the disregard of the crowd as it gathered around, and he lifted his hand to pluck the badge from his vest, then thought better of it.

Doctor Spooner was taking charge. He was giving orders for men to take the bodies to the funeral parlors; Vic Canny he wanted in his office, right away. There was a bare chance the Rocking V man might live.

Jed watched him. A sullen anger replaced his shame. He was the law. Didn't these men know it? He'd show them he was the law!

He went back inside the office and took the double-barreled shotgun down from the gun rack. He found shotgun shells in the desk drawer and he loaded both barrels.

The crowd was dispersing when he stepped outside. Those who were still about stopped and watched him with puzzled interest.

Jed walked determinedly across the street, punching the dust with his peg leg. He put a hand on the knob of the lunchroom door, turned it, and put his shoulder against the door.

The door banged hard against the wall and the glass panel shattered. Jed stumped in, lifting the shotgun as Kip, slumped on the stool, turned at the sound.

'I'm the law, kid!' he said. His voice was hoarse and unreasoning. 'You seem to have forgotten that. I asked you about Tom—'

'I don't know about Tom Gallen,' Kip cut in roughly. 'I told you that before.'

'You told me to mind my own business!' Jed sneered. 'Wal, I'm mindin' it. You'll talk to me, kid. You'll talk or you'll rot in that cell I got ready for you!'

Kip's face went hard. 'Put that down, Jed!'

'Wouldn't you like me to!' the older man snarled.

'What is yore game, kid? Who you with? First time I saw yuh, yuh wasn't packin' a gun. Now you show up wearin' a Colt.'

'*Put that down!*' Kip's voice was bleak.

'I gave you your chance, kid!' Jed snapped. 'Now I'm jailin' you!' He cocked back both hammers. 'You comin' along peaceful, or you want trouble?'

Kip looked at Sally. She was in the line of fire; her face was pasty white. He nodded and rose from his stool. 'Take it easy,' he said coldly. 'You might hurt somebody with that thing.'

'Put yore hands over yore head!' Jed

ordered harshly. 'Keep them there! An' walk slow. You know where my office is!'

Kip walked out and across the street. Jed stumped behind him, his eyes glittering, feeling his importance. He saw eyes on him, and his shoulders went back and a tough look settled on his lined face.

Inside the office, he stood by while Kip unbuckled his gun belt and dropped it on his desk. He opened the door to the cell block, unlocked a door, and motioned Kip inside.

He closed the door behind Kip and locked it. His face held anger and a deep hurt pride. 'Mebbe I seem like just an old fool to you, kid, not worth talking to. But you'll talk to me when I'm ready, kid. You'll tell me what happened to Tom Gallen or, by Jehoshaphat, I'll see you hang!'

Kip turned away from the man. There was no use explaining to this hopped-up cripple who was blind to everything but the memory of the way Kip had ignored him. The smaller the man, Kip thought cynically, the more violent his reactions to little things . . .

He settled back on the cot and stared up at the ceiling.

*       *       *

Sellout waited tensely. The shooting between Verne Mathis and the Rocking V gunslingers could only mean the start of a range war that

158

could destroy the valley.

Jed Peters, suddenly unsure of himself, sent a garbled message to Sheriff Henry Alterman at Meridian asking for help. He scribbled the message in the office and sent Tad Myers' boy to the depot five miles away to hand it over to the telegrapher. Then he went out and bought himself a quart of whiskey and proceeded to get drunk.

Doctor Spooner took over. He sent a message to Monte Cozzens, explaining what had happened in town and requesting that Monte use his head and not let this obvious feud break out into more senseless killing. He sent the same sort of message to Brent Westwood.

Brent came to town alone. A tall, grave-faced man, he had Verne's body laid out in the crude pine box which served as a coffin and had it loaded on his light wagon. He tried to see Kip Nunninger, but Jed Peters, half drunk and ugly, levelled his shotgun at him and told Brent no one was gonna see his prisoner.

Brent left town without talking to Kip Nunninger. He drove to the ranch with Verne's body in the back of his wagon and with a feeling of anger and helplessness nagging him. He had trusted this rough, hard man who had been his foreman as he had trusted few men in his lifetime; Verne's death hit him hard.

And now he faced the dismal prospect of trying to hold back the men who had worked for him—those hard, grim men who had taken Verne's orders and respected him. He agreed with Doctor Spooner that retaliation on Rocking V was senseless. But would he be able to stop his riders?

Monte Cozzens took the news of Chinook's death and Vic's critical condition more calmly. He had never trusted the two men. He had hired them because they looked like tough hands, and because he knew he would need fast guns when the break came with Three Dot.

They had not fitted in with Rocking V. They kept arrogantly aloof from the other hands and took orders from Cornel Tate, his foreman, with what amounted to outright insolence. More than once they had been in town when Cornel had thought them riding line. The last time had been more than Cornel could take. He had fired them. And Monte had been glad to pay them off.

They had no longer been Rocking V hands when they had come to town today, but Monte Cozzens did not bother to explain. He had not liked Verne Mathis either, and he figured that Chinook and Vic Canny had done him a good turn anyway.

With Cold Springs in his possession, Monte had what he wanted. He intended to keep it. If Three Dot tried to take the Springs back they'd have a fight on their hands. Otherwise he'd be content to settle things as they were.

Monte Cozzens was a driving man and he knew how far he could go. But he didn't figure on Kansas. And though the outlaw boss had worried him somewhat, he had not reckoned Kansas in on Antelope Valley.

This afternoon he sat on his broad porch with a bottle of cold beer at his feet and a cigar in his mouth and made his plans.

*       *       *

Behind the low mesa to the northeast, a group of hard-faced owlhooters were holding a last minute conference. Seven men were grouped around Kansas.

'We'll go over it once more,' the stocky outlaw boss said harshly. 'We'll hit Cold Springs first. Monte's got two men standing guard over the wire, according to Chinook. We'll run them down, cut down the wire. Then we'll hit Rocking V. Remember, we're not trying to wipe Monte out. We'll hit him hard, hurt him. We'll make him so blind mad he won't be able to think straight or see straight.' He turned to the slim Mexican at his left. 'You and Tony burn down the barn. Don't expose yourselves—we don't want anyone hurt or killed. We want Monte to think it's Three Dot raiding him . . .'

They nodded. Kansas stared out over the country. The sun was low over the horizon. It would be gone in an hour.

This was what he had planned for more than a year. If it worked, he'd own Antelope Valley before the end of another month.

He drew his neckerchief up over his broken nose. 'Let's ride . . .'

They hit Cold Springs at sunset. There were two Rocking V hands standing guard over the recently erected wire barrier. They kiiled both of them, tore down the barbed wire strands, stampeded Rocking V beef.

Two hours after dark they hit Rocking V itself. They caught one man in a crossfire as he sprinted from the well toward the bunkhouse, and dropped him. They poured lead into the house, into the bunkhouse. They broke every window on the place: They set fire to the big barn; they stampeded the Rocking V remuda out of the corrals.

When they withdrew they left the sky behind them glowing brightly . . . and a stunned and shaken spread trying to understand what had hit them.

'I'll give Monte until morning.' Kansas chuckled during a momentary halt in their return to the Sleepers. 'He'll have every man able to ride in saddle. And he'll ride for Three Dot!'

At the dry fork above Devil's Creek they paused again, slipped bandannas from their faces. Kansas let his hard gaze search the darkness. A light, glowed faintly, far off to the south; it caught his attention, and old memories came to life, again. He had a sudden impulse to see her again, and he gave in to it. He turned to Keno.

'Take the men back to the hideout, Keno. Stay clear of Yellow Horse, just in case things break wrong. I'll meet you back there by tomorrow night.'

Keno had caught his look to, the south. He nodded slowly. '*Si*, Kansas. We'll wait—'

Kansas waited until they had faded into the night. Then he turned his cayuse and headed for the Havison spread. He rode easily, following a trail he had taken before. He heard a train mourn in the darkness, far away and faint, and he thought of his brother Kip with an odd detachment. The kid was out of the way—probably back in Frisco now. He'd send him some more money later—might even send for him when he owned Three Dot.

He came to the rise of ground behind the ranch and dismounted, ground-reining the black. He walked down. By the stars it was almost midnight. Meg and Nora would be asleep. But Malvina would probably be awake . . .

He reached the dark shadows flanking the barn. He heard a snort in the darkness and he turned, his voice sharp. 'Down, Cerebrus. It's only me.'

He heard the old hound's tail thump a few times in tired greeting. Then it was quiet.

He found the lantern on the nail just inside

163

the door. A hen clucked sleepily. The wood match he lighted on his thumbnail showed his broad face, flattened nose, light gray eyes, hard mouth. He was a man so sure of himself he never questioned his motives.

He stepped out into the yard and waved the lantern. It was an old gesture, one he had not used in more than six months. But tonight he felt the urge to see Malvina again.

He thought he saw something move against the upper window. There was a period of waiting and he began to grow impatient. Then the door opened softly and a shadow moved across the porch and came down the steps.

He put the lantern down and Malvina came into its light. She was taller than he, and she looked like a man with her hair piled up on top of her head, tucked under an old hat. But she was a woman, with a woman's tenderness. She came up to him now, her eyes dark and questioning and bitter.

He said insolently: 'You ain't changed a bit, Malvina. Still wearing pants, still sloppy as ever.' But he reached out and pulled her to him and kissed her, holding her hard in his muscular arms.

She fought him. Some shreds of pride in her rebelled at his callousness; at his arrogance in assuming that she would always be here, waiting, ready to receive him at his pleasure. She fought him and finally broke away from him.

164

He scowled. 'What's the matter? You sick?'

'Yes,' she whispered harshly. 'I'm sick of myself; sick of allowing myself to be treated like this by you—a murderer and a thief. A man who can't show his face among decent people!'

He reached out and caught her arm, his hard fingers hurting her wrist. 'What's come over you?' he demanded. 'You didn't have to come out. Why did you?'

'Because I'm weak,' she whispered, and her anger and her pride collapsed. She was too long alone, too long the sole strength and support of Broken Quirt. She wanted help. She needed a man's help, a man's comforting arms at the end of the day.

He kissed her again, and she returned the kiss.

It was Kansas who pushed her away. His face held a contemptuous sneer. 'So I'm a murderer, not fit to associate with decent people, eh? What about you? Your sister Meg?'

His voice was cold water, chilling her. She stiffened. 'Kansas! You wouldn't tell—'

'Why not? She killed a man, too. Killed him because he preferred a lunchroom waitress to her. Shot him in the guts and brought him home, bleeding to death, in back of her buggy. And you buried him, didn't you, Malvina? Up on that hill. Not even near your own folks. Brent Westwood would like that, wouldn't he?

165

His own son, not fit to be buried beside that drunkard, Gunner Havison—'

She reached for him with clawing hands. But he brushed her aside and slapped her— slapped her hard, splitting her lips, rocking her head back.

'Keep away from me,' he sneered. 'I came here to do you a favor. I don't know what came over me. I don't even want to touch you now.'

He turned and left her. She was still as stone, white as a sheet. The shame in her was deeper than pain. She made no move. He went up the dark hill behind the barn, and after a few moments she heard the hoofbeats of his horse as he rode away . . .


## CHAPTER THIRTEEN

Monte Cozzens wiped blood from his face. A splinter from the window framing had cut his cheek just under his left eye. He stood on the porch of his ranchhouse, trembling with a rage that was like a fever.

The enormity of what had happened was just getting through to him. He watched his barn burn down to the ground, while his men, some of them wounded, fought to save the sheds near it. The ranchhouse was far enough away and upwind of the barn to be safe. But the horses in the corral had broken out and stampeded.

In the red glare of the fire Monte's face was a savage mask. Cornel Tate, his ramrod, a dour man standing six foot seven, shook his head in angry puzzlement.

'Didn't think Brent Westwood was that kind, Monte. Darn uppity, bein' a Britisher an' all. But it was him who kept Verne Mathis from ridin' down on us before. Can't figger it out now, unless Westwood didn't like his foreman gettin' boxed in a gunfight an' killed.' He looked at the fire and scowled. 'Mebbe you should have passed the word along that Chinook an' Vic wasn't workin' for Rockin' V when they killed Verne—'

'Heck with that!' Monte snarled. 'They raided us! That's what counts! Well, we'll give them a taste of their own medicine!'

He stepped down into the yard and called his men together. They made a grim ring around him, outlined by the dying fire.

'That was Three Dot who hit us!' he said harshly. 'Couldn't be anybody else! They started this fight, but by Jupiter, we're gonna make Westwood wish he never had! I'm telling you all now. Any man who doesn't think he can fight Three Dot, speak out now! I'll pay him off and he can ride, tonight!'

No one took his offer. The raid had killed two men and wounded two more. There wasn't a man there who wasn't boiling to get even.

'We'll ride then,' Monte decided, 'soon as we can round up the horses. We'll hit Westwood the way he hit us—only we'll hit him harder!'

It took them four hours to get ready. There was no sleeping that night. They worked grimly, rounding up the scattered horses, breaking out extra ammunition. They didn't leave a man behind. They rode out of Rocking V in force; even the wounded went along.

They hit Three Dot just before dawn. They caught the big ranch asleep and they hit it hard. When they left several of Three Dot's outbuildings were on fire and three men were dead. Four more were wounded.

Brent Westwood lay on the steps of his house with a bullet-smashed leg. He lay there while men went about the grim business of fighting the fires that still raged, and taking care of the other wounded. He watched this with cold and bitter eyes, knowing that he could no longer hold back these men of his . . . knowing that there could be no rest for him now until Rocking V was smashed . . .

\*       \*       \*

Malvina Havison came into Sellout around midday. She rode a bay horse like a man, and the .38 lay in its holster at her hip. She rode into town and turned up the wooden ramp of the Straw Stables.

168

Old John Straw was having his siesta on the bench in the narrow shade of the barn. The thumping of iron hoofs on the ramp woke him. He brushed his floppy hat up from his eyes and scowled at the woman who looked down at him.

'Come for yore mare, Malvina?'

She shrugged. There was a strange look in her eyes; she was like a sleepwalker seeing things with an inner vision. There was a bruise on her cheeks and her lips were puffed.

'I'm looking for a man named Kip Nunninger,' she said. 'He came to town yesterday.'

Straw nodded. 'Yup.' He eyed her closely now, and his suspicions of Kip seemed confirmed. 'Stole that mare of yores, didn't he? Figgered him for a bad one, Malvina. Fooled me, too—when he first showed up. Funny-lookin' button—'

'Where is he?'

The stableman knuckled the gray stubble on his jaw. 'Wal—he's in the calaboose right now.' His voice sounded puzzled. 'Ol' Jed's gone loco, I reckon. Since Tom Gallen's been gone he's walked around like some Confederate general, givin' orders an' polishin' that tin badge of his—'

'Never mind about Jed,' Malvina interrupted coldly. 'Where's Kip?'

'I'm comin' to him,' the oldster muttered. 'Vic Canny an' Chinook, two of Monte

169

Cozzens' new hands, whipsawed Verne Mathis an' killed him yesterday afternoon. Right up the street, in front of the law office. This kid yore lookin' for—he was in the lunchroom. He popped out a-runnin' an' called Chinook an' killed him. The other one, Vic—he's still in the doctor's house. Hear he's dyin—'

'You say Kip's in jail?' Malvina's voice was strange.

'Yup. Ol' Jed marched him out of the lunchroom behind a shotgun an' into a cell. Won't let anyone see him, either. He sent the sheriff down at Meridian a message, then locked hisself in the office with a quart of whiskey an' got mean drunk.'

Malvina sniffed. 'Then Kip's still there.' She dismounted and turned to the stalls where Vanity, recognizing her, shrilled her greeting.

'Saddle her for me, John?'

The old stableman nodded. 'Sure thing, Malvina.' He grumbled as he worked. 'Looks like thet range war we been expectin' is gonna break loose now. Thet Limey Westwood ain't gonna let Rockin' V get away with killin' his foreman—'

He looked at Malvina, but the Havison woman wasn't interested. There was a wooden quality to her waiting. He finished saddling Vanity and turned to the bay. 'You gonna leave him here?'

Malvina shook her head. 'I'll need him, too.' She mounted Vanity and rode out, leading the saddled bay. She turned up the dusty, sun-beaten street and tied up at the law office.

Jed was slumped over the desk when she tried the door. It was locked. She could see the old codger through the dirty window. She rattled the door, and he stirred and his thick voice came to her. 'Go 'way!'

Malvina drew her gun and smashed the glass. It jangled harshly in the stillness. And it brought Jed lurching to his feet. He grabbed his shotgun and came to the door and slid the bolt back. He opened it, his red-rimmed eyes ugly, his mouth twisting harshly. 'I said I'd shoot—'

The muzzle of Malvina's .38 jabbed him painfully in the bulge above his belt. He gasped, and his eyes rolled, and he let go of the shotgun. It dropped at his feet, and Malvina kicked it inside the office and pushed Jed back. She closed the door.

'I want your prisoner,' she said. 'Don't try your play-acting on me, Jed. Get Kip out of that cell. Then you can go back to sleep.'

He started to sputter, saw the look in her eyes, and the fight went out of him. His stomach was queasy with the whiskey he had drunk and his head pounded. He turned and staggered away toward the cells.

He came back with Kip. Malvina was holding out the gun belt and Peacemaker she had found stuffed in one of the desk drawers.

'You wanted Kansas, Kip,' she said harshly.

'I'll show you where to find him!'

Kip looked at her, studying the wooden set of her plain face, the hard light in her eyes. He saw the bruise and the swollen lips, and a dozen questions came to him and were put aside. There would be time enough to get answers later.

He buckled the belt and holster about his flat waist. He nodded grimly. 'I want Kansas.'

She stepped back and opened the door. A small group of men and some women were clustered outside. They fell back when Kip stepped out, followed by Malvina.

'Take the bay,' the Havison woman said. 'It's going to be a long ride.'

Jed came to the door. Malvina turned to him. 'Don't try anything foolish, Jed . . .'

He was too sick to try. He watched them wheel away from the tie-rack and raise dust out of town. He leaned against the door, his mouth slack, and cursed bitterly.

\*　　　\*　　　\*

Vic Canny regained consciousness for the first time since the shooting in front of the deputy sheriff's office. He lay on the doctor's bed, although he didn't know it, and the ceiling came slowly into focus. And with it came pain, twisting his thin face, causing a shuddering cry to break from his lips.

The woman who had been standing by left

172

the room and called Doctor Spooner. He came into the bedroom and bent over Vic.

'Doc—the pain! Stop the pain!'

Doctor Spooner said: 'I'll see what I can do for you.' The man was dying, and another hypodermic would not matter now.

'Chinook!' Vic's voice was a thin questioning cry.

The doctor turned to him. 'Chinook's dead. So is Verne Mathis. That ought to please you.' He regretted it immediately. A doctor had no right to pass judgment.

'Kansas!' Vic's voice was a wild cry. 'Doc—it was Kansas' doin'. Me an' Chinook worked for him.' His eyes sought the doctor's face. 'I don't care now, Doc—not afraid of him. Me an' Chinook took the job with Rockin' V to be on the inside. We—'

The doctor waited, holding the hypo in his hind. His eyes met those of the woman, and he nodded slightly.

'Me an' Chinook tried to kill that Englishman Westwood. Kansas hired us to do it. But we run into that kid at the water stop—and he fouled us up—'

'You say you worked for Kansas?' The doctor leaned over the dying man. 'Who is he? What does he want?' 'Antelope Valley,' Vic answered. His body stiffened at the burning pain in his stomach; he set his teeth against it. 'Doc—the pain—please, Doc—'

Doctor Spooner nodded. He lifted Vic's left

173

arm and injected the hypo into his triceps.

'Wants Westwood's Three Dot spread,' Vic gasped. 'Usin' thet phony Judge Weller as a front to buy out the Britisher. Kansas started the trouble between Rockin' V an' Three Dot . . . He's gonna raid Rockin' V soon. Wants Monte Cozzens to think it was Three Dot doin' it . . .'

He closed his eyes. His breathing quieted. 'Funny thing, Doc . . .' His voice was dreamy now. 'Chinook always said he'd have a share in Three Dot. 'Cause he knew what happened to Brian Westwood. Only he an' Kansas know—' His voice trailed off and his breathing was barely perceptible. Doctor Spooner knew he'd never awaken.

He straightened up and laid the needle aside. He was a short, rotund man who had seen death often and never took it casually.

'Martha—you heard him?'

The woman nodded.

'I must ride out to see Westwood,' Spooner decided. 'I want to tell him about this. And Monte Cozzens, too. It's still possible to avert the trouble between them . . .'

He drove away in his buggy a scant fifteen minutes before the Westbound Limited stopped at the depot. Three men got off. The heavy, middle-aged man with the star on his coat was Sheriff Henry Alterman. The other two were Arizona Rangers.

They led saddled horses out of the baggage

174

car and rode into town. It was late afternoon. They rode directly to Tom Gallen's office and found Jed snoring, his face on the desk.

Sheriff Alterman shook him with a rough hand. 'Jed!' he said. 'Wake up!'

Peters raised foggy eyes to the three men standing over him. He had finished his second bottle of whiskey and his breath was enough to jolt a man at ten paces. 'Broke jail,' he mumbled. 'Not my fault—pulled a gun on me. Havison gal—pulled a gun . . .'

Sheriff Alterman let him go with a snort of disgust. 'Reckon he won't be any help to us for a long while,' he growled.

Benjamin Crawford pushed through the crowd around the doorway and came inside. 'Good afternoon, Sheriff,' he greeted Alterman. His tone was reserved; he was still smarting over the way the sheriff had ignored his requests for action. 'I see you finally got here.'

'I came as soon as I could get away, Mr. Crawford,' the sheriff said. There was no cordiality in his voice. He waved to the men flanking him. 'Steve Fetterson and Nat Ames, Arizona Rangers. Gentlemen this is Mr. Benjamin Crawford, banker.'

They shook hands.

'Perhaps you can fill us in on the details,' the Ranger called Fetterson suggested. He was a rangy man, about twenty-five, with level gray eyes.

175

Crawford nodded. 'I'll tell you what I know, gladly.'


## CHAPTER FOURTEEN

Kip had been this way before, but it seemed different now. The land was no longer strange and hostile and he knew what lay ahead. The Sleepers came out of the afternoon, rising bare and desolate above the long talus slopes, and then they retreated into the blue shadows as the sun dropped behind the western hills.

They rode in silence most of the way, Kip Nunninger and Malvina Havison. He had questioned her at the first opportunity, but she had not replied.

They were in the hills when she finally took a breather. He edged the bay up close to her, his face hard. About them the long rocky slopes were dark and brooding in the fast-growing dark.

'You know Kansas!' It was not a question; it was a flat statement.

She nodded. 'Quite well, Kip. I guess you could call him my sweetheart!'

He looked at her with a sudden frown, but she was staring into the darkness. There was a deep and burning hurt in the woman, and he suspected that Kansas was responsible. A woman scorned? Somewhere he had read that phrase—it explained Malvina tonight. He shrugged.

'He's no good, Kip.' Her voice was low, flat. 'He's a killer, a thief. He wants only one thing, and he'll do anything to gain it. He wants to own all of Antelope Valley. He wants land—a lot of land. Strange, isn't it, Kip? Kansas never owned much in his life. He came out here and the land got him. And now he wants all of Antelope Valley.'

Kip listened quietly, letting her speak.

'I offered him Broken Quirt,' she said. 'There wasn't anything I wouldn't have done for him. He's strong, Kip; he's got drive. He could have turned that strength to more honest ways, perhaps. I really don't know. Maybe there are flaws in all of us—flaws we're born with. Maybe Kansas could never be anything else than what he is: an outlaw; a man who'll always take what he wants, without regard for others.'

Kip shrugged. 'I don't know about flaws,' he said. 'And I don't care what Kansas wants. He killed my brother. I want to know why, before I kill him for it.'

He didn't see the sad look in her eyes, or the hurt that crimped her lips. 'Maybe he'll tell you, Kip,' she murmured. 'I'll want to hear it, too.'

He straightened abruptly, impatience sounding in his voice. 'You know where to find him, you said. How did you find out?'

177

'I followed him one night, after he left me. He didn't know.' She made a small gesture with her hands. 'My father was a mountain man, Kip. He taught me a lot of things. Things not ordinarily taught young girls. Things a man might teach his son, perhaps. But I was always a tomboy . . .' Her voice held a strange defiance. 'I followed Kansas to his hideout. He never knew.'

Kip said: 'We're wasting time then.' He started to rein the bay away, but Malvina reached out and put a hand on his arm.

'Kip—you're going to be hurt tonight. But just remember this. Kansas is a killer. Remember that when you see him!'

Kip frowned. 'Sure I'll remember. Didn't I tell you he killed my brother!'

She sighed. 'I guess he did . . . a long time ago.'

Fred Nunninger, alias Kansas, counted the money out on the table in front of Judge Silas Weller. 'Twenty thousand,' he said. 'After yesterday Westwood will be glad to sell to you and clear out!'

Keno, standing behind Kansas, grinned. 'You pay him with money we take from the bank, eh, Kansas? Maybe it is some of Westwood's own money, no?'

Kansas shrugged. 'You know what to do, Judge?'

Weller nodded. He had bags under his eyes and his tongue was furry. But fear cleared his

178

head. 'I ride into town and put this money in the bank. Then I ride out to see Mr. Westwood and try to close the deal—'

'Not try,' Kansas cut in ominously. 'You'll close it!'

Judge Weller nodded. 'I give Westwood a draft for twenty thousand, tend to the legal details, see that I get a bonafide bill of sale, properly witnessed. Then I let you know.'

'Stay off the liquor!' Kansas warned. 'Stay away from it until the deal is closed and I take over. You've got a loose mouth when you're drunk.' He leaned across the table, his eyes boring into the judge. 'You spoil this thing now and I'll kill you. I'll kill you the way the Apaches killed . . . slow. Keep remembering that, Judge!'

Judge Weller nodded hastily. 'Sure, sure, Kansas. I won't make any mistakes.' Then he hesitated, forced a smile to his lips. 'You promised me five thousand dollars when I finish this job. I'd like—'

'You'll get nothing now!' Kansas snapped. 'When the Three Dot is mine you'll get your money!'

Weller sighed. 'I just thought I'd mention it.' He rose and tucked the money into his wallet and slid the billfold into his inside coat pocket: Keno followed him outside.

Kansas paced the small back room of the hideout shack, his thick shadow sliding noiselessly over the rough board walls. He should be hearing from Vic and Chinook any time now. Their job was to hang around until Monte made his raid on Three Dot, then come here. They were overdue.

He paused and looked at the dingy room he had called home for more than a year. Malvina's accusation echoed faintly in his ears: '. . . A man who can't show his face among decent people . . .'

He should have killed her. She was the only person outside of his own men who knew he was Kansas, the outlaw. And when he became Fred Nunninger again, respectable owner of Three Dot, she would still know. And he knew now that he or Keno would have to make another visit to Broken Quirt soon.

Keno came back into the room. 'That was a lot of money to turn over to that windbag,' he said softly. 'You think he'll do as you say?'

Kansas nodded. 'He'll do it.' He was not worried about the judge running out on him.

Keno shrugged. 'The boys are restless. They want to go to Yellow Horse for some fun.'

Kansas waved his hand. 'Sure. But you stay, Keno. I got something I want to talk over with you.'

The killer nodded quickly. 'I'll be back *muy pronto*, Kansas.'

\*　　\*　　\*

Out in the night Kip and Malvina waited. They

had left their horses in a small, dark hollow and crawled to the entrance to the box canyon. They waited now while Malvina whispered: 'They have a guard out somewhere, Kip. Up on that rock ledge, I think. We'll have to get by him somehow.'

The sound of a buggy coming through the canyon passage interrupted her. They flattened down on the low rise above the dim trail and watched Judge Weller drive out of the deep shadows. There was enough light from the stars to make him out.

From the twenty-foot ledge Malvina had indicated, a voice hailed the judge. He waved stiffly, without looking back.

He drove by, passing less than twenty-five feet from Kip and Malvina. He drove on into the darkness, and the sound of his passage faded away into the night.

Kip whispered: 'I've got an idea how we—'

The clatter of hoofs stopped him. Six riders loomed up out of the canyon darkness. They jeered a greeting to the guard on the ledge, and he answered them with sullen displeasure.

Malvina said: 'Probably going into Yellow Horse—'

Kip nodded, watching the riders fade among the hill shadows. 'Maybe Kansas was with them,' he muttered.

Malvina shook her head. 'I know Kansas, even in the dark. He wasn't with them.'

Kip settled down. 'We've got to get by that

181

guard. If you're game, I have an idea how we can do it without giving him a chance to warn those still back there.'

Malvina listened. 'Sounds all right,' she agreed.

'Count to fifty, slow,' he instructed. 'Then go ahead . . .'

He got up on his hands and knees and moved away as she started to count. He kept to cover and the deep shadows and made it to the base of the ledge without incident.

He seemed to wait a long time before Malvina appeared on the trail. She walked slowly, as though she were lost. But he knew that she was in plain sight of the man above him.

He heard the guard stir, and pebbles sifted down, making a small sound in the night. Then the man's voice rang out harshly. 'Whoa down there! What you up to?'

Malvina paused. She looked up and lifted her hands. 'I'm looking for Kansas,' she said. 'He told me to meet him here, but I got lost . . .'

More pebbles sifted down as the guard started down the ledge. Kip crouched. The lanky man dropped to the ground less than ten feet from where Kip waited and turned toward Malvina, his Winchester held ready in his hands.

Kip jumped him. The guard caught the scuff of Kip's boot and started to turn; his startled features came around in time to meet Kip's fist. He grunted, and his hands went up, and the rifle clattered to the ground. His knees buckled and Kip hit him again, a quick one-two. The outlaw sagged in the middle and fell on his face.

Malvina came to them, her face tense. 'What about him?' Kip asked grimly.

'We'll tie him,' she said.

Five minutes later they left the stirring guard wedged between rocks, tied hand and feet with Kip's and Malvina's neckerchiefs. Part of the man's shirt was stuffed in his mouth, a gag he objected to with muffled protests.

Malvina hesitated. Then her hand came up to the bruise on her cheek and the memory of last night burned deep. She whispered harshly: 'He's there, Kip—waiting . . .'

\*     \*     \*

Kansas turned as Keno came back inside the small room. 'Glad they're gone,' he said heavily. 'I got a special job I want to talk over with you.'

Keno nodded. He was quick, Kansas thought—quick-thinking as well as fast with those guns of his.

'That Havison girl,' Kansas said, 'the big one. Looks like a man. She runs Broken Quirt.' He knuckled his jaw thoughtfully, his grin sly. 'Remember, I told you about her?'

'*Si.*' Keno nodded.

'She knows who I am,' Kansas said. 'Savvy? When we move down to Three Dot, she'll still know. That ain't good, Keno. A woman talks. I want you to fix it so she can't talk. You're good at that sort of thing. Fix it like you did with that deputy, Tom Gallen. Ride down to Broken Quirt one night and—'

Keno whirled at the sound of a quick step behind him. Malvina Havison came through the doorway, the .38 in her hand holding them both.

'No need to ride that far, Keno,' she said. 'I'm right here. And you're so right, Kansas. A woman talks, especially a woman scorned and insulted—' She laughed at the look on Kansas' face, but it was shaky laughter and there was a hint of nervousness on her face.

'I've brought you a visitor, Kansas. Someone you know well—or should!'

Kip came into the room behind her. His face was white. He faced his brother across the table, seeing the unpleasant surprise in Fred's eyes. He felt a knot tighten and squeeze his insides until the hurt ridged his jaw.

'So you're the outlaw Kansas?'

Fred took a deep breath. 'You fool!' he, snarled. 'I thought I had you packed and on your way back to Frisco! Even stuffed your pocket full of money—'

Kip's hand dug into his pocket; he flung the bills across the table top. 'You should have let

184

me alone,' he whispered. His face was gray now, and his voice was thin and uncertain. 'You should have let me be. I would have left you on my own, Fred, believing what that woman in Yellow Horse told me: that you had gone away. I would have liked that better, Fred. I liked the memory of you as I knew you in Frisco better—'

Kansas glanced sideways at Keno, who was balanced on his toes. The silence made an ugly gap between them.

'What are you gonna do about it, kid?' Fred's voice held an arrogant sneer. 'Hide behind this woman's gun?'

'I'm going to take you and him back to Sellout,' Kip said. His voice was dead. 'I'm going to turn you over to the law.'

Kansas shook his head. 'You don't know me, kid. Guess you never have.' His voice lifted suddenly, in harsh command. 'Get him, Keno—' And with that he lunged sideways, his hands reaching for his guns.

Malvina shot him three times.

Kip had whirled around at Fred's cry; he caught Keno with his first shot and slammed the gunslinger against the wall. Keno's gun hammered once, and Kip felt a burning tear in his side. Kip fired again, and Keno sagged and slid down. The Colt slid out of his hand.

Malvina was standing where she was, rigid, staring at the man she had shot. Kansas had fallen forward across the table top. He tried to push himself up; his fingers clawed among the bills Kip had thrown at him. Veins bulged at his temples. He looked at Malvina, his voice thick, clogging in his throat. 'You . . . you . . .' Then he slumped forward and lay still.

Silence crept back into that smoke-hazed room. Malvina turned slowly and dropped her gun; her face was crumpled broken, and old-looking in the lamplight.

'I told you you'd be hurt, Kip,' she whispered.

He stared stonily. Strange how the one thing he remembered about his brother now was the phrase out of his last letter: ' . . . They wear big hats in this country, kid . . .'

'Let's get out of here,' he said finally, 'before the others get back.'

\*       \*       \*

They made the town of Sellout by mid-morning. Three horses trailed them. The bodies of Fred Nunninger and Keno lay across the saddles of two; the trussed guard lay across the other.

They were dead tired. The ride back seemed to take an eternity, was a half-remembered torture. Each rode with his own thoughts, his own bitter memories. At a point where Malvina could have turned off for Broken Quirt, Kip had suggested she go home. She had shaken her head. There were things she had to finish now. The law would have to know what had happened to Brian Westwood.

They rode into town at the moment a posse was forming in front of the law office. Three strangers, one of them with a star on his coat, were in charge.

The posse opened up to let them ride up. Sheriff Alterman came down the steps toward them.

'I'm the sheriff,' he said. 'We were just about to ride to Yellow Horse after Kansas—'

Kip turned and made a motion to the dead man behind him. 'That's Kansas,' he said wearily.

Sheriff Alterman frowned. 'Come inside, both of you.' He turned to the mounted men. 'Maybe we won't be riding at all, but stand by.'

Inside Tom Gallen's office, Kip and Malvina told their story. The two Rangers listened quietly. Sheriff Alterman shifted uncomfortably at the question Malvina put to him.

'There's been too much trouble already,' he said. 'Luckily we got here in time to stop more killing. Doctor Spooner told us about Kansas' part in it as he heard it from a gunman named Vic Canny. Then, this morning, Judge Weller drove into town and we picked him up. He's in the cell back there now. He told us the rest of what we needed to know. We were just about to ride out when you arrived.'

'About Meg,' Malvina insisted, 'you haven't

told me what will happen to her. She killed Brian in a fit of jealousy—and paid for it. She'll be paying for it until she dies.'

Sheriff Alterman nodded. 'That will be up to Mr. Westwood,' he said stiffly. 'But I don't think he'll press charges. You can't commit a—'

'A girl who's lost her mind,' Malvina finished bitterly.

Kip rubbed the palm of his hand across his eyes. 'You need me here, Sheriff?'

Alterman shook his head. 'Not right now. But don't leave town son. We'll have to get your testimony on the record.'

Kip shrugged. 'I'll be here. Across the street—having a cup of coffee.'

The sun was in his face as he stepped outside. He didn't look at the body of his brother across the saddle of the big black horse. He stepped down into the street and walked slowly toward the curtained window where the letters BONNIE BONNET LUNCHROOM were painted.

In time, he thought, he'd come to like this country . . .

We hope you have enjoyed this Large Print book. Other Chivers Press or G.K. Hall & Co. Large Print books are available at your library or directly from the publishers.

For more information about current and forthcoming titles, please call or write, without obligation, to:

Chivers Press Limited
Windsor Bridge Road
Bath  BA2 3AX
England
Tel. (01225) 335336

OR

G.K. Hall & Co.
295 Kennedy Memorial Drive
Waterville
Maine 04901
USA

All our Large Print titles are designed for easy reading, and all our books are made to last.

p